BARREN LAND SHOWDOWN

FORMERLY: BARREN LAND MURDERS

Luke Short

G.K. Hall & Co.
Thorndike, Maine

Published in 1996 by arrangement with
Kate Hirson and Daniel Glidden.

G.K. Hall Large Print Paperback Collection.

The text of this Large Print edition is unabridged.
Other aspects of the book may vary from the original edition.

Set in 16 pt. News Plantin by Rick Gundberg.

Printed in the United States on permanent paper.

Library of Congress Cataloging in Publication Data

Short, Luke, 1908–1975.
    [Barren land murders]
    Barren land showdown / by Luke Short.
        p.   cm.
    "Formerly, Barren land murders."
    ISBN 0-7838-1462-3 (lg. print : lsc)
    1. Large type books.   I. Title.
[PS3513.L68158B37   1996]
813'.54—dc20   95-24374

BARREN LAND
SHOWDOWN

Chapter One

The storm broke suddenly, and it boiled out of the east as if its cold and buckshot snow were hurled from a gun. The little knot of people waiting for the weekly mail plane on the riverbank first turned their back to it, then broke and scrambled back across the drifted flats to Lobstick, leaving only those who had business to meet the plane. They were five men, and a dog team and sled that would ferry the mail up to Lobstick and the post office.

When, minutes later, the muffled drone of the plane sounded overhead, a sixth man broke away from the shelter of some stacked oil drums and walked out to join the others. He was a tall man whose worn and shapeless parka did not hide the breadth of his shoulders or the long length of his legs. His bush dress — parka, moccasins, beaver cap, mittens on a cord looped through the parka collar — set him apart from the others, who wore sheepskins or mackinaws and laced boots.

He came up to one man whose identity was given away by the yellow outseam on his dark blue breeches, paused, and said above the wind, "He could use a radio beam today."

Corporal Millis turned. The recognition in his

pale eyes and broad face came slowly. He studied the taller man, the lean black beard-stubbled jaw, the green eyes deep-welled under black brows, and his first thought was that this was a sober young man, almost unfriendly. And with that came recognition, and he shucked off his mitten and put out a square hand.

"Hello, Nearing. Haven't seen you for months."

"Since before freeze-up," Frank Nearing said. They shook hands.

"How're things up on Christmas Creek?" The Corporal's broad face twisted in a grimace. "What a name for that God-forgotten hole! How was the fall hunt?"

"So-so."

Corporal Millis looked up at the sky then. The plane was a misty shape above them as it hurtled downwind for its circle into the wind before landing on the immaculate snow of the river. Frank Nearing watched it too, and Corporal Millis regarded him obliquely, carefully. This was the young chap who had come to him in early summer, a silent Cree Indian for a companion, and had announced his intention of prospecting and trapping up the Wailing River around the Christmas Creek country. Millis had not seen him since, and he was faintly troubled at the change he noticed. There was a kind of ferocious reserve in the man's eyes, and a lean, wolfish, weathered look that a man gets who is working harder than he should. Millis was curious.

Frank Nearing, aware of that look, gave Millis

8

time for it because a policeman is supposed to know his people. Then he glanced at him, and Millis' look slid away.

"You must be pretty anxious for your mail," Millis observed.

"No. My partner's coming in on this plane."

"That a fact?" Millis' voice was unconcerned, but his interest was sharp. He was a good man, Frank knew, and Frank wanted to satisfy him.

"You three will find pretty thin pickings up in that country."

"We'll make our grub in fur this winter. Mostly we want to prospect back in the McFarlane country next summer."

"It's a big country," Millis remarked, and the tone of his voice told Frank that he was satisfied for the moment. The hardest part of this was to come.

The plane came down in a long slow glide into the wind, its skis touched the river, and the snow foamed up from them like water from the prow of a boat. It taxied over toward them, and the mail dogs suddenly started barking and snarling. When the plane stopped some yards short of the bank, the group broke and streamed down to the river.

Frank left Millis on the bank and went down too. A sudden uneasiness was on him, and his heart was pumping with a controlled excitement. This was the moment he had been dreading — and for an audience he had the one man he must impress with the casualness of the thing.

The door of the old Bellanca opened, slammed shut in the wind, and was forced open again and hooked. Then a man stepped out, and Frank's attention was narrowed to him for an instant. He was lean, dark, young, and thoroughly drunk. He missed the step, pitched into the snow, and was hauled up laughing by two of his friends, who took his baggage from the pilot and guided him away. Frank ignored him.

His attention was all for the man who next stepped out, and his hard eyes studied him with a faint excitement stirring them. This man was a burly giant in boots and sheepskin. This was his man.

Frank called, "Hello, Lute!" and waited, for he had never seen the man before.

The big man's reactions were expert. He smiled broadly and called, "Hello, fella," and then they met and shook hands.

The stranger had sensed the game. His solid heavy face was smiling easily, and he looked at Frank with a feigned fondness that was nevertheless searching.

"How's Uncle Joe?" Frank asked.

"Fine. Sent his regards. You're looking good, Frank — a little thin, but good."

And all this time Corporal Millis, his blue eyes veiled and watchful, was seeing and hearing this and not wondering.

The pilot handed out Lute's luggage, and Frank took it, then guided Lute up the bank to Corporal Millis.

10

"Corporal Millis, this is Lute Westock."

Millis put out his hand and said, "So you're the new partner Frank's been telling me about? Well, you picked a cold roost, you three."

Westock smiled. He had a blond, scrubbed look about him, and an iron command of himself. "Nice to meet you, Corporal," he said. Nothing more. Frank knew then with a vast and sudden relief that he was not going to overplay his hand.

"Let's get out of this blast," Millis said. He turned toward the road that came off the river and crossed the hundred yards of drifted flats to enter the town of Lobstick.

Heads down against the driving wind that made talk almost useless, they walked abreast up the trail. Ahead of them, propped unsteadily between two larger men, was the drunk. He wore new boots whose slippery soles did not help his footing, and a long blanket coat. His largest companion carried a bulging duffel bag over his shoulder.

Westock said to Frank, "Who's the rummy, Frank?"

"I don't know."

Millis said, "He's Bruce McIvor, a worthless young pup. He went out to join up with the Air Force, and was rejected."

They were soon at the head of Lobstick's main street. Two dozen gaunt-ribbed log stores with false fronts faced each other across the ice-rutted road.

The trio ahead turned left, heading for the alley, while Millis and Frank and Westock continued

11

straight, aiming for the street.

There was a sudden commotion, and Frank looked over to notice that the drunk had fallen again. This time he pulled one companion down with him.

This man's voice, rough and savage, said, "Quit it, Bruce. Damn it, stand up."

Millis saw it, looked away, and said to Lute, "How're things outside?"

Frank didn't hear Lute's reply. The two men had picked up the drunk and were taking him down the alley. A sack, which had dropped out of the duffel, lay on the ice.

Frank stopped, saw they had not noticed it, then walked the few steps over to the sack and called, "Hold on, there!"

He knelt to pick up the package. Its container, ordinary grocery sacks doubled, had burst on the ice, and a fine white powder inside spilled out. Frank picked it up gingerly and walked toward the three, who were coming back now. They stopped when Frank came up to them.

"You dropped this out of your pack," Frank said.

For one brief second, the three of them stared silently at the sack. Then the biggest man said quickly, "Looks like borax. Here, dump it in my pocket."

He looked across at Millis, who was still walking across the road beside Lute and still talking, then held his mackinaw pocket open. Frank deposited the sack in it and dusted his mittens briefly, suddenly aware that they were watching him in utter silence. He looked at the big man, whose soft dark eyes were alertly curious in his big square-jawed face. The man said curtly, "Thank you," dismissing him.

As he caught up with Millis on the sidewalk, Westock was talking about the news from Korea. Another safe subject, Frank thought, and he knew suddenly that there was nothing to fear. Westock knew his part.

The steady snow was softening the outlines of this unlovely town squatting between the Raft River and the black bush rising tier on tier back into unmapped bush and muskeg. A hundred years ago the fur brigades had boiled into it at the end of the staggering portage from the land-locked lakes to the north, and they had howled and sung here before facing the wild lower reaches of the Raft's white water. A company governor had dined here off the silver plate that was carried for him in his fleet of bateaux. He had watched the lobstick out on the point cut in his honor, and had smiled bleakly at the childish Indians who were honoring him and whom he was bleed-ing of beaver and pelts in exchange for rusty guns. That lobstick, a tall spruce shorn of all its limbs except a broad tuft at the top, had long since been undermined and washed away by the savage floods of the Raft. The timbers of the old stockade were fallen and rotted now. The steamboat had found safer waterways to the west, and the airplane had found a newer way. Even the company had deserted the post, and the shell of it fell away, leaving this tight stubborn core of a handful of stores that lived from the furs gleaned from the wilderness. That core, Lobstick today, was remote, lonely, unmentioned, forgotten save by the police, by the church, and by the weekly mail plane. The nights were darker here.

At the two-story log hotel down the street, Millis left them, after shaking hands and wishing them luck. Frank led the way through the hot lobby and mounted the stairs to his sparsely furnished room. Once the door was closed, he and Westock faced each other.

"Did I do all right?" Westock asked.

"Perfect. He's got us pegged as two mining men out of a job."

Frank slipped out of his mittens and parka, peeled off his beaver cap, tossed them both on the bed, and knelt in front of the rickety commode. He opened it, brought out a bottle and two glasses, and rose.

He confronted Westock, who was holding out a slip of paper. Westock said, "One thousand dollars deposited to your account in the bank you specified."

Frank pocketed it without looking at it and poured two drinks while Westock shed his coat, and then he handed one glass to Westock.

"Luck."

"To our new partnership," Westock supplemented. They drank.

Frank settled his loose frame on the table and

put his shoulders against the wall. Drawing out cigarette papers and pouch, he rolled a cigarette with broad and big-knuckled hands, and studied Westock with a lazy and careful attention. In repose his face had a leaned-down soberness, an unsmiling gravity. His eyes, deep-recessed under thick black brows, were alert and cold and shrewdly calculating. As soon as Westock sank onto the bed with a satisfied grunt, Frank said, "Now that you're in here and the police aren't curious, just who the hell are you, Westock?"

There was a blunt and almost arrogant toughness in his manner of speech that brought Westock's gaze up to him in silent and questioning appraisal. Then Westock rubbed his palms together, because it was chill in here, and he asked, "What did Joe write about me?"

"That you wanted a place to hide. That you were willing to pay two thousand dollars for it, and that you weren't a criminal."

"That all?"

"No. He described you."

And badly, Frank reflected. Joe had written that this man he was sending was big and blond. Frank had pictured him as jovial, loud, and profane, like Joe Phillips himself. But this man was not. He was one of those rare big men whose every act is done with a small man's grace, but his alert pale eyes were utterly humorless, sober, watchful. His head was small, well shaped, firmly modeled, and strong at the thick cheekbones, and his hair was finespun and the color of dry corn

15

shucks. Under a worn plaid windbreaker his shoulders were tremendous and thick. His manner of smoking a cigarette was almost ceremonial in its deliberation. Something about his scrubbed, sure hands, his alertly observant manner told Frank that in his thirty-odd years Lute Westock had never been dirty and had never been denied much.

Lute said, "Joe didn't know much more than that himself."

"But I want to," Frank said flatly.

"You mean you've lied to the police for me. Now you want to know what I'm trying to hide?"

"That's about it. And your name."

"There's no reason why I should tell you that," Westock said gravely.

"I'm the judge of that."

"Pardon me, but you are not," Westock said calmly, with an iron courtesy. "Observe that I'm not trying to deny Westock isn't my name, but my real one is no concern of yours, Frank. While you may get angry about it, I don't think you'll go to Millis and turn me in."

A faint admiration for this man's gall came to Frank, and with it a slow anger stirred. Frank fought that down, knowing his nerves were a little thin and his temper quick. The wind hammered at the windows.

Frank's face was a little hot, but his expression did not change. He said, "Suit yourself about the name. But you'd better suit me about the other

16

— why you're hiding."

"That's simple. I was once too well married."

Westock smiled faintly at Frank's scowl, and went on, "I had a lot of money once, before my divorce. My alimony to my wife was generous. Now, with these new taxes, I can't afford to pay it. She insists, and has the backing of the court. So I transfer my property to a partner, refuse to pay alimony, get a court summons, and then hunt a place to hide. When my wife finds she can't touch my property or jail me, she'll compromise with my lawyers. Meanwhile, I'm paying two thousand dollars for food, shelter, and complete anonymity." He spread his clean hands. "That's all."

Frank looked at him with quiet cynicism, leaned forward, dropped his cigarette on the floor, ground it out, then said quietly, "No dice."

"Meaning what?"

"Your story stinks. You'll have to do better than that."

"I'm sorry you think so. It's the truth."

"You won't give me the right one?"

"You've got it."

Frank rose slowly and came over to confront Westock. His big hands were on his hips, and in his taciturn face was a deep and savage intolerance.

He had his mouth open to speak when a firm knock came on the door. He looked at it, annoyed, then crossed over and opened it.

A girl was standing in the corridor. She said,

"Are you the man up on Wailing River?"

"Yes."

"I'd like to talk to you."

Frank stepped aside and the girl entered the room. Westock rose as she came in. She was not a tall girl, and she was wearing a solid-color blue flannel shirt open at the throat, a heavy tweed skirt, and laced field boots. Golden hair lay in twin thick braids around her head, and beyond that Frank did not have time to look at her, except to notice that she was out of breath, uncertain of herself, and so excited that her blue eyes were shining. She carried a sheepskin coat over her arm. She lifted it now, brought out a new pair of mittens, laid them on the commode, then said to Frank, "I'm going to make a trade with you."

She saw Frank's parka on the bed, turned it over, and picked up his mittens. "That's a fair exchange, I think," she said, and started for the door. Lute was ahead of Frank. Lute brushed past her, slammed the door, and leaned against it, an expression of wariness on his face. The girl was at a loss for a moment. She looked over at Frank and asked, "Will you ask him to let me go?"

Lute said mildly, "Forgive my curiosity, but you were listening at the door, weren't you?"

"I was not!" the girl answered angrily.

Lute smiled, his eyes faintly ugly. "I believe the practiced hotel eavesdropper always carries some clean towels over her arm in case she is surprised. Maybe you're green at this."

18

Frank said, "Easy, Lute."

Lute looked beyond the girl to Frank, his eyes hard. "Of course she was listening!"

The girl stepped back from Lute then and turned slowly to face Frank, a kind of pleading in her eyes.

"You'd better talk," Frank suggested.

"I just traded you mittens. That's a fair exchange, isn't it?"

"Maybe," Frank said slowly, "I don't like new mittens. Maybe I don't like mysteries either."

The girl bit her lip. "Will you burn them if I leave them?"

"No. Why should I?"

"Oh, why do you have to be so stubborn? I'll leave these new mittens! If you won't let me take the old ones, then promise to burn them!"

She looked at Frank; he was regarding her with a deep and puzzled bewilderment. Then she turned to Lute. There was more than suspicion in his face; it was an actual dislike.

And he did not move to get out of the way. He said, "How much did you hear, my dear?"

Frank looked angrily at Lute, but Lute was watching the girl. And she had suddenly made up her mind.

"All right," she said brusquely, and spoke to Frank alone. "I suppose it's too much to ask you not to repeat this."

Frank didn't answer.

She said, "Those mittens of yours have strychnine on them."

Frank, bewildered, came over and took his mittens from her. Lute looked on as Frank turned them palm up; a white dust still clung to the worn hide and filled the creases. The package he had picked up, the strained look of those three men by the alley all came back to him then, and he said quietly, "Sit down."

The girl sat on the edge of the bed. To Lute's questioning glance, Frank said, "That drunk and his friend dropped a package. It broke, and I picked it up." He said to the girl, "Who told you?"

"My brother. He was the drunk. He was afraid. You could have killed a couple of your dogs tonight when you fed them. You might even have got it yourself."

Frank nodded. "Your brother peddles the stuff?"

"No!" the girl said shortly, and then added, less sure of herself, "That is, I don't think so. Oh, I don't know why he did it, except that he does those things and always has! But I'll make him destroy it — all of it."

"He traps?"

"That's what's queer; he doesn't. He's no bushman, and he hates the bush and is afraid of it. I think he was bringing it in to sell to some of these bush tramps who are too lazy to work at trapping and would rather poison their fur." She paused now, a kind of stiff pride in her face. "Are you going to tell Millis?"

Lute, who had been listening carefully to this, said, "That depends, Miss —"

"McIvor. Kelcy McIvor."

"Are you quite sure you didn't hear anything beyond that door?" Lute asked.

Frank's voice rapped out sharply, "Shut up, Lute!"

The girl came to her feet in the onrunning silence, her manner brisk. She said calmly to Frank, "I don't think you'll tell Corporal Millis. Your friend here is worried that I might have overheard something. Perhaps I did. Apparently both of you have something you don't want known." She looked levelly at Frank. "In case you go to Millis with this story, I propose to go to him also. I'll ask him to take a little care in checking your past history, both of you. Do you understand?" To Lute she said in a contemptuous voice, "Your blackmail works both ways, my friend. Now please let me go."

At a nod from Frank, Lute stepped aside and opened the door. The girl paused in it and looked back at Frank. "The man from Wailing River," she murmured gently, almost mockingly, with a deep-running impudence. "You're just as unfriendly as you look, and there's not much mystery left, is there?"

"Was there ever?" Frank asked coldly.

The girl nodded. "We're human here, and curious about you. But I'm not any more. Because when two people blackmail each other into silence, it's almost certain to be for shabby reasons. Mine is smuggled strychnine. I don't think yours is any better."

She went out then, and Lute softly closed the door behind her. In the fading daylight, Frank and Lute regarded each other in utter silence.

Then Frank said in a thick voice, "I didn't take you for a clumsy damned fool. You are."

Lute didn't say anything, and Frank went on, his voice hard and edged with temper, "That girl didn't hear anything. But your ham actor's hush-hush has got her suspicious now."

Lute said curtly, "That's my worry, Frank, not yours. I'm the one who has to be careful!"

"You bloody fool," Frank murmured, his voice cold with scorn. "I've lived in this country since summer. I've talked to nobody, seen nobody, kept them away from me. I've done it for a reason — a good reason. Beside it, your secret doesn't count a damn!"

Lute said, with a puzzled contriteness, "I didn't know that, Frank."

"You know it now," Frank said bitterly. "Why do you think I'm hiding a man I don't know anything about? It's because I need your money enough to risk prison to get it. Did you think about that?"

"How could I? I don't even know whether you'll hide me."

Frank wheeled, disgust in his face, and walked over to the window. He stood looking out on the darkening town, and the snow drove steadily outside, clawing at the eaves of the room and hollowly shaking the windows. His face was bleak, angry, strained.

He heard Lute move, and then say in a matter-of-fact voice, "I still don't know. What are you going to do about me?"

"I'll hide you," Frank said slowly. Then he turned and peered through the gloom at Lute. "Damn you, Westock! Keep your mouth shut from now on. Let me talk, let me play this my way. If you don't I'll break you in two, fella! I mean it!"

Lute was quiet a long moment, and then he said dully, "Right. You're the skipper."

Chapter Two

Lobstick's post office was in one walled-off front corner of Robb McIvor's big store. Kelcy waited until the mail was racked and the usual people were clotted about the radio waiting for the news at six o'clock, and then she sent her father home for supper. As soon as he was gone, she got a coat and slipped outside.

It had been dark almost two hours now, and the thick relentless snow blurred the lights from the stores across the street. Kelcy put up her parka hood and sought the road, then traveled downstreet to the hotel and beyond. The gasoline lamps from the stores laid a bright lattice in the clean snow, but Kelcy did not notice this tonight.

At a dingy restaurant whose windows were frosted almost to the top, so that only the legend "Star Café & Hotel" was visible on the glass, she went in. The steaming heat smote her in the face like a soft pillow. A half-dozen men eating at the counter paid no attention to her. The girl behind the cash register saw her first, and over her full-lipped sulky face came an expression of surprise.

It was gone when Kelcy saw her and came over and asked, "Is Saul around, Bonnie?"

"Upstairs," Bonnie said tonelessly. She watched

Kelcy walk past the counter seats, and Bonnie was smiling faintly, crookedly. She was a dark, handsome girl, full-breasted, with sullen vivid lips and deep brown eyes that were coldly and cynically curious now. When Kelcy opened the door beside the kitchen door and mounted the steps, Bonnie started for the stairs, then changed her mind and came slowly, thoughtfully back to the cash register.

Halfway up, the stairs turned at right angles and opened onto a narrow lamp-lit corridor running the length of the narrow building.

A man was standing by an open door in front of one of the rooms; he closed the door now, and walked down to Kelcy. It was the square-jawed burly man in whose coat pocket Frank had deposited the "borax."

Kelcy said wearily, "How is he?" as she brushed her parka hood back and shook off the snow.

"Just woke up, and he can navigate," Saul Chenard said. He came up to her, his big thick body dwarfing Kelcy's. He put a hand on her arm and said gently, "Kelcy, how do you put up with this?"

Kelcy smiled faintly. "I don't think I could if it wasn't for you, Saul."

Saul shook his head in somber sympathy, and the lamplight caught the sheen of his tight black curls and softened the hard line of his face. He had full pouting lips that went strangely with his rugged face and big body. He sighed. "Hell, I can't do anything with him. I'm not much help."

"You can hide him at times like this."

"Thank Bonnie for that," Saul said. He smiled faintly. "She likes him."

"We all do," Kelcy said wearily. "That's what makes it so hard."

Saul hesitated and then said casually, "What about the two rover boys?"

Kelcy grimaced. "It didn't work, and I had to tell them. But I don't think they'll tell Millis."

"No?" Beneath Saul's casualness was an alert attention.

"They thought I'd been keyhole-snooping at their door. They were talking about something very private. Anyway I pretended I had overheard, and told them that we'd both better forget Millis. They agreed, and pretty quickly, too."

Saul laughed silently and shook his head in admiration. "You're a wonderful girl, Kelcy — a lot better sister than that lovable no-good brother of yours deserves."

Kelcy only smiled and said, "May I see him?"

Saul led the way back into a clean, bare room containing only an iron bed, a dresser, a desk, and one chair. Bruce McIvor, his reckless swarthy face blurred and heavy with sleep, looked up to regard Kelcy from where he was sitting on the edge of the bed.

She came over to him and silently combed his black hair with her fingers. "Hit the deck, Bruce. We're going home."

"What's Dad said?" Bruce asked.

"I told him you were so disappointed at being rejected that you took a drop too much, and were ashamed to show up until you were sober."

A wry humor lighted Bruce's thin face, and then faded. "What about — the strychnine?"

"That's fixed too," Kelcy said levelly. "I got to Nearing before any harm was done. He won't tell."

Bruce came unsteadily to his feet and shook his head. He had to steady himself by grabbing the foot of the iron bed.

Kelcy watched him with a dismal look in her eyes. "Bruce, how could you be such a fool as to bring that stuff back?" she asked miserably.

"No sermons," Bruce said sharply. He looked at her, the wildness in his face close to breaking through, and Kelcy bit her lip. Then Bruce went over and threw himself in the chair, and presently he bent over to pick up his boots.

Saul shifted his feet faintly and said, "Kid, you'll take a sermon from me and like it. The only reason Millis hasn't got you in the clink now is because you're lucky."

"All right," Bruce said, not even looking up.

Saul's voice bore down now. "I mean it. That little poison idea of yours laid a nice train of powder. If it's discovered, you'll go to jail. Kelcy will be dragged in it for hiding knowledge, and so will I."

Bruce was bent over, lacing his boots. His hands paused, holding the laces, and for a moment it was utterly quiet. They were waiting for his temper to flare up. Finally he said, "All right," calmly.

Kelcy said with relief, "Hurry home now, Bruce. No more liquor. I've got to get back to the store."

Bruce didn't say anything, and Kelcy smiled at Saul and said good-by. When they heard her descend the stairs, Bruce looked up.

There was a rash and wicked anger in his eyes. "You bloody fraud," he said thinly to Saul. "Don't do that again — not ever."

"Don't be a damn fool," Saul said calmly. "I had to. Kelcy doesn't suspect where that strychnine's going, and she mustn't."

"So you blame me for it."

"You get your cut out of the fur," Saul pointed out coldly. "Besides, no harm's done. She believes she got it all. By tonight, the boys will be out in the bush with the rest of it. Why all the yelping, anyway?"

Bruce stood up and stamped his feet into his boots. Then he looked at Saul. "I just don't like it," he said quietly. "Another thing I don't like."

"You're a regular prima donna tonight, kid," Saul said dryly.

Bruce looked at him steadily, his dark eyes smoldering. "I overheard that soap you handed Kelcy out there in the hall. I'm warning you, Saul. Stay away from her."

Saul's face changed subtly, settling into harder lines. He said nothing and Bruce went on calmly, "I'm neck deep in this cheap racket of yours.

28

I don't mind it. But keep Kelcy out of it. And keep away from her or I'll kill you!"

The sound of footsteps on the stairs silenced him. In a moment Bonnie sauntered through the door. Bruce's eyes lighted up at sight of her. She came over and kissed him lingeringly and said, "Down off your binge, honey?"

Bruce grinned, and the smile lighted up his dark, brooding face. "Down to rock bottom. Been good while I was gone, Bonnie?"

"Better than butter," Bonnie said, smiling.

Saul murmured matter-of-factly, "If you want to catch your old man before he gets back to the store, you better light out, kid."

Bruce put on his mackinaw and picked up his fur cap. He kissed Bonnie again, patted her curves, and said, "I'll be in later." To Saul he only nodded on his way out.

When he was gone, Bonnie put her shoulders against the wall and folded her arms in front of her. "Another talk with the Duchess," she sneered. "Was it thrilling?"

"Lay off," Saul said curtly.

"Who asked her to come here?"

"I didn't. She came to send the kid home." Saul's soft eyes were sullen. He said, in a soft, downbearing voice, "I don't like that kid's hands on you, Bonnie."

"Who told me to make a play for him?"

Saul looked at her a moment, then turned to go. Bonnie came up to him and put her arms around his neck. "Saul, why do we fight like

29

this?" she asked softly. "Why don't we get out of here?"

Saul patiently untwined her arms, and Bonnie looked at him bitterly. "How much money do you want, Saul?"

"More than I've got," Saul said dryly. "Beat it now."

"Kiss me, and I will."

Saul kissed her. When he was finished, Bonnie's eyes were soft and happy. Saul laughed mockingly, and listened to her trip down the stairs.

Then he went out into the corridor and down to the end room and entered it. Three men were playing poker at a table under the overhead kerosene lamp, using pennies for chips. They were unshaven, uncombed, and in worn and ragged coveralls, the uniform of a bush trapper. Three walls of the room were filled with double-tiered bunks. Ostensibly, Saul ran a cheap hotel and restaurant, catering to the trappers and Indians in from the bush. They could put up here and have their dogs fed for fifty cents a night. In reality it was a blind for Saul Chenard's real business. He employed six men, seasoned bushmen, quiet, furtive men who seldom saw the post. He furnished them with the best dogs money could buy, and with strychnine. From before the first snow until the fur began to rub, they traveled fast and hard and light, penetrating into the far lakes, the bush country, the muskegs. Behind them, they left a trail of deer and moose and caribou carcasses around which they scattered poisoned bait to attract the fur. At the end of their long swing to the edge of the Barren Land, they would return, picking up the fur that had fed off the carcasses and had died. White fox, red, silver, cross, lynx, mink, weasels, birds — anything that would touch meat — was killed. They could wipe a country clean of fur in a season with the fine white powder they carried. And their haul of fur, baled and hidden when they entered Lobstick, was fabulous. They were a scourge of which the police were ignorant, because they stayed far off the trails of the other trappers.

These three, half of his crew, waiting for the strychnine Bruce McIvor had brought in today, greeted him quietly and went back to their cards. Saul pulled a chair over to the table and put a foot on it, then folded his arms and rested them on his knees. "Joe, you ever get around to Wailing River?"

One of the men looked up from his cards and shook his head. He was a half-breed, and had the patient, inscrutable look of the Indian, which had conquered the white blood in him. "No fur that way."

"I want you to move out that way this trip. Starting tonight. And get this, and get it good. You'll use traps on the Wailing. No poison, you understand?"

The breed nodded. He put down his cards now, attentive, and protested, "But there's no fur, Saul."

"I don't give a damn. I want you to find out

31

about that bird Nearing up there."

"All right."

"I want you to crowd him, Joe. If you find any of his sets up there, jerk his traps. Make trouble. Claim you've trapped the Wailing for ten years. Muss him up."

Joe looked dubiously at Saul. "Maybe he don't muss up."

Saul smiled. "He'll stay out of trouble, Joe. I can promise you that. He's not anxious to have Millis take a good look at him, and he'll take his riding."

"O.K.," Joe said. Then he added, "You want the Wailing for us, Saul?"

"Hell, no," Saul said. He straightened up and swung the chair away. "I'm just curious about Nearing. He's in the lonesomest damn spot in this country. I want to know why, and if my hunch is right, I can stop his mouth any time I want."

"Stop his mouth?" one of the other men asked.

Saul scowled, and then laughed. "That's right. He saw that poison the kid brought in this afternoon, and he says he won't tell Millis. I wonder why."

Chapter Three

Frank didn't like Lute. He came to this conclusion after a day of being with Lute, watching him buy his outfit, talking to him, observing him. He just didn't like him, and it wasn't wholly because of what had happened the afternoon before. There was something about his new partner, a deep arrogance overlaid by courtesy, a humorless skepticism, a deep reserve that Frank could neither break through nor understand.

That night in his hotel room Frank lay sleepless. He was remembering Lute as he bought his outfit — rifle, moccasins, parka, bedroll, duffels, mittens, everything — and he was suspicious. For a man who had been rich once, Lute knew bush ways. He had shown the unbending taste of a bushman in his purchases. It was a little thing, and it troubled Frank.

During those sleepless hours, Frank again weighed his decision, as he had weighed it before. It was not too late to back out from this new partnership. But the money, the two thousand dollars that he needed so desperately, held him to his decision. That knowledge rode him and drew his nerves wire thin. There was trouble ahead with Lute. He was tough, secretive, with a temper close to the surface. And sooner or later

Frank must tell him his own secret. He could not hide it, like Lute could hide his. That secret that he had shared with one man, Charlie Cree, his Indian man, had grown a part of him. Sooner or later, he must share it with Lute. When? Before he slept he decided to wait until they got to Christmas Creek. That was the place. And drowsing off, he schemed of ways to bind Lute more tightly to him.

Before daylight next morning they were headed up the Raft. It was a tough river, and the higher it went, the tougher it got. A half day's travel above Lobstick, where it was crowded between towering rough-faced walls so steep that the snow did not cling to them, there was a crack in the north face of the wall. Gaunt black ramparts broke away to reveal an opening, snow-floored, narrow, serene. This was the Wailing. Entering it, a man dived into a gloom that never saw the sun, himself and his dogs dwarfed by the ugly porphyry cliffs, and his spirit was awed.

The shore line was barren, for the race of its waters and its rock face had won over a stubborn nature, and nothing grew here. Below the ice, the rumble of the boiling waters was constant, filling the canyon mazes with its whisper.

It was a little after noon, with Lute ahead breaking trail with the small trail shoes, when they reached the junction of the Wailing and the Raft. The snow still held, boiling out of the east at their backs, laying its swirling curtain on the trees, weighting them down, wiping out all the game

34

tracks, and making this a new country. Lute paused there at the mouth of the Wailing, waiting for Frank, who whoaed the team and walked past them. His dogs were five matched sons of a Coronation Gulf husky mother, big-boned and rangy and raffish-looking. They lay in their traces, tongues dragging, tails wagging.

When Frank approached, Lute pointed to the snow. "Someone turned up here yesterday. That your man Charlie?"

Frank didn't even look at the snow. "For a rich man divorced from a rich wife, you read bush sign pretty well, Lute."

Lute's bland face didn't change. "Don't I? But I wasn't talking about that. You told me you never saw a stranger on Christmas Creek. What about this?" He indicated the trail.

Frank knelt by the toboggan trail that swung in the crack of the cliffs. His own trail, old, was faintly discernible, hugging the near shore. A second trail, fresher, missed his, but swung into the Wailing also. It puzzled him. The Indians were afraid of the Wailing; the trappers shunned it, for not until a man got to its headwaters would he find good fur country. It gave Frank a faint uneasiness, which he did not show to Lute.

He rose and said dryly, "Do you drive dogs too, Lute?"

"I'll try."

"Give me your shoes. I'll go ahead."

Lute toed out of his snowshoes and gave them

to Frank. "Is it Charlie's trail?"

"I don't think so."

They traveled the rest of that day and long after dark up the Wailing, oppressed by its walls, its chill cold, and its echoing sound. Occasionally a tangle of driftwood thrust up through the ice, and even these were sinister reminders of its force, for they were as thick as a man's body and gnawed and shredded by the power in this restless river below them.

Long after dark, when the canyons fell away and there was wood, they camped. Next morning they woke to a different country, bleaker, rougher, colder, lonely as the stars. Black spruce snarled the twisting river shore, and the man who had been before them still kept to the river. He had found Frank's trail, had hit every portage over the long points, and at midday they found his camp of the night before. Frank studied it with a growing uneasiness. The man had six dogs, big ones. Little things, like his choice of a camp, the way he had rigged his tarp lean-to, the wood he had chosen for fuel, the way he chained out his dogs, told Frank many things.

And then Frank found the man's first set. It was a fox set, just at the head of a portage in timber so thick a fox traveling the river would take to the trail. Frank didn't bother to hang the trap — the universal warning to a trespasser in the North. He sprang the trap with a stick. In midmorning he found one of his own traps hung.

Working farther up the Wailing in the dry, driving snow, Frank found a dozen more of his traps hung. He said nothing to Lute, who was driving the dogs. That was another cause of uneasiness, too. He wondered again with a growing cynicism what sort of bargain he had made, and knew it was too late to back out now.

Where a feeder creek from Whitefish Lake came into the Wailing, Frank stopped again, and this time he felt his suspicion harden. The toboggan trail still clung to his own, which kept to the Wailing. A man who was up here to trap would have headed over for Whitefish and east. This man was headed for Christmas Valley.

He left the Wailing soon, where the trail took to the bush, clinging to a series of jack-pine ridges that rose higher and higher. Presently, close to dark, he paused on the lip of one ridge, breathing hard from the pace he had set, and waited for Lute, a wild impatience within him.

When his big blond partner came up beside him, Frank pointed. "There's the shack below. You go ahead, and I'll take the dogs. The trail's tricky. Hurry it, fella." There was controlled haste and impatience in his voice.

Ahead of them and below, in a deep valley tucked away in the folds of this bleak country, was the tiny black spot of a cabin in a clearing among the spruce. It almost hugged the steep barren rock slope of the opposite side, and looked as lonely as a ship on an ocean. Frank watched Lute as he studied it briefly, and then Lute said,

"It's lonesome enough, all right." He turned to Frank. "Only who's your caller?"

"I'm going to find out."

While he rigged the sled's tail rope to serve as a rough lock, Lute descended the twisting trail. The slope was not sheer, but a sled out of control could smash into a thousand pieces here. It picked its descending way by a series of hairpin turns through the stunted spruce and jack pine, until finally it flattened out, four hundred feet lower, onto the floor of Christmas Valley.

Frank was on Lute's heels as they reached the valley floor, and Frank curtly handed over the dogs to him and set out at a long trot. The trail threaded through a tall stand of timber, slipped into a stream, turned up it, followed it north, then came to a clearing by the cabin.

When Frank reached the clearing, he paused again. The trail of the toboggan went right to the door of the long, low shack.

Frank ran then. He passed the front of the shack, noting that the door was open, and then he halted at the corner of it, regarding an old drifted-over trail that aimed at a jut of rock in the steep slope and disappeared behind it. This trail showed no tracks, but Frank didn't seem satisfied. He took to the trail, skirted a point, and hauled up at the drifted mouth of a tunnel in the rock face of the cliff. Ten feet into that tunnel there was a heavy timbered door padlocked to a spike driven deep into the living rock. He paused there, breathing hard, and saw the padlock undisturbed. Nor were there any new marks on the ancient plank door. The intruder hadn't been here, hadn't seen it.

He heard Lute from behind him say, "What is it, Frank?"

Frank heaved a deep, shuddering sigh and brushed past Lute. "Let's see what's plundered, first."

Together they went into the cabin. It was a big affair, and its main room was wider than it was deep. The north end of it was the kitchen, with a small stove and crude cabinets. The south end was the bedroom, with a table between a pair of double-tiered bunks. In the back wall was a door, for which Frank headed. It led into another room, empty save for a workbench, a small furnace built into one corner, some retorts, some scatterings of coal, some bins of ore samples.

Frank closed the door then, and regarded the living room again. Dirty dishes littered the table, grease coagulated on them.

He cursed softly and looked at Lute, who was regarding him with alert curiosity.

"Where's Charlie?" Lute asked.

"Trap line, probably." A sudden decision came into his voice. "Get a fire going, Lute, while I unload the sled. I'm hittin' the trail again."

He lugged the load in from the sled. In the gathering darkness he went out to the open cache, a high rack in the rear of the shack out of reach of the dogs, took down a hindquarter of moose meat, and threw it in the cariole. The dogs whined hungrily, waiting to be unhooked. Frank paused by the leader and said, "Not yet, fella."

He went inside then. Lute, curious but silent, had lighted the lamp, and the water was boiling. From the grub box Frank pulled out some bannock and broke off a hunk, and then Lute put the teapot on the table. His cap and parka off, Frank, still standing, ate the half-frozen bannock and swigged the tea. The somber look on his face had deepened. Lute watched him curiously.

Frank said suddenly, "Wondering what it's all about?"

"Who wouldn't?"

"I haven't got time for much of it," Frank said curtly. "But you'll get enough to understand." He bit off a chunk of bannock and talked around it. "See that tunnel door I went to first?"

"It's a mine, I suppose."

"There's about a hundred thousand dollars' worth of ore in sight there," Frank said calmly.

Lute's eyes widened a little. He said, "Nobody'll steal that. Why the secret?"

Frank arrested the tin cup halfway to his lips and looked levelly at Lute. "Because this isn't my claim."

For a moment they didn't speak. Then Lute said curiously, "Claim-jumping, Frank?"

"I was waiting for that," Frank said sardonically. "No, partner, I'm not claim-jumping. I didn't dig that tunnel; I didn't throw up this shack. This claim and this shack and this valley were abandoned."

Lute was puzzled. "If that's so, I still don't see why you're so worried."

Frank ripped off another hunk of bannock and talked rapidly. "Know how a claim is abandoned, Lute?"

"No."

"The law favors the original staker. He has to put in only sixty days' work on a claim the first two years, and ninety the third. And what he does in one year is allowed to carry over into the second. That's what happened here — only the bird who staked it missed the third year."

"And when is this third year up?"

"Almost two months ago."

"I don't get it, then," Lute said. "You're clear to stake it, aren't you?"

"Except for the three-month extension he's allowed by law, I'm clear," Frank said grimly. "The law gives him an extra three months before his claim is forfeit. If he can show sickness or a hundred other excuses within three months, he retains title."

"And if he doesn't?"

"Then the recorder marks the claim canceled, and I can step in and restake it."

Lute was silent a moment, carefully regarding Frank, who was swigging the hot tea in grim and hurried silence. "I see," he said softly.

Frank didn't look up, but went on with his eating.

"And you're wondering who's paid you a call, because if he saw that tunnel he can tip off the original claimant."

"He didn't see it, though," Frank cut in. "There weren't new tracks to it. But if people figure they can come in here to look me over any time they want, they will see it. And once they do, they'll tip off the original claimant and he can come back and claim the work I've done, prove there's ninety days' work in it, get his patent, and then mine a fortune out of it," Frank finished swiftly. He set his cup down and looked levelly at Lute.

"That's why I need your money, Lute," he said matter-of-factly. "The ore is free milling. With a small crew, I can fly some out and show the assay, and the machinery company will give me all the credit I need."

Lute said curiously, "How'd you get onto this?"

Frank was pulling on his parka, and he smiled faintly at Lute's question. It was the only time Lute had seen him smile, and then it was a twisted one. "For three damned summers," Frank said, "I waded muskeg and fought flies back toward the height of land. I prospected this whole formation. Two years ago I came to these diggings. I saw what had happened. Up on the slope there, this prospector had found color against a porphyry-diorite dike. He figured the pay-off would be at the foot of the dike. It was a vertical dike. He came down here, put in his tunnel, and found a porphyry-diorite dike. He cut upcasts and crosscuts around the foot of it, but he didn't find anything. He left the place then, and I'll bet he wondered what had gone wrong."

"What had?"

Frank smiled again, again crookedly. "He'd worked on a false dike, same formation. The dike he'd spotted up on top wasn't vertical. A hundred feet down, there was a slip, and it took a forty-degree slope toward the north. He'd mistaken a false dike for the real one. When I found that, I came down to his diggings, put his tunnel on through to the real dike, and found the ore body."

"You did that in secret?" Lute asked slowly.

Frank picked up his mittens and cap, nodding, and then he raised his somber gaze to Lute. "Try it sometime. Try portaging a summer's grub over the height of land and traveling at night. Try single-jacking instead of blasting, because you're afraid of the noise. While you're at it, try hunting moose with a bow and arrow, like Charlie did, for fear of a gunshot being heard. Try doing the tail end of a summer's work on blueberries!" His eyes were hard and stirred faintly with anger. "You've been sulking, Lute, because I got tough in Lobstick when you tipped that girl off that maybe we were hiding something from Millis. Now you see why. I've worked here a whole summer and part of a winter, and nobody knew my name, except Millis. They thought I was a sorehead trapper." He finished bitterly, "I'm not playing for white chips, fella."

Lute's heavy face flushed a little. He asked slowly, "You think she's tipped off whoever made this visit?"

"I'll find out," Frank said. He put on his cap, and then eyed Lute steadily. "Let's get this settled before I leave, Lute."

"Whatever it is, go ahead."

"In case you've got any ideas about getting word to the wrong people about this, I wouldn't." He paused, letting that sink in. "I don't know why you're hiding, Lute. I don't care. But if you talk to anyone about Christmas Valley and what's going on here, I'll turn you over to Millis. He can find out why you're hiding, and who wants you."

The muscles in Lute's jaw flicked faintly, but his eyes were steady. "That's fair enough. One thing more. If I'm turned in, Frank, I'll blow up this little mine-stealing deal for you, too."

Frank nodded grimly. "We know where we stand now, don't we?"

"Exactly."

The dogs outside started a savage barking then, and Frank went out swiftly. He grabbed the whip from the sled and cracked it savagely over the leader's head. The dogs stopped barking. Frank, Lute behind him, listened. They heard the brittle brushing sound of a toboggan on the snow, the pad of dogs' feet. And then, out of the darkness, a team limped into the clearing and started barking.

A man heaved himself slowly out of the cariole, and Frank ran over to him. "What's the matter, Charlie?"

"Nothing much," Charlie said.

Lute saw only a slight man of medium size who spoke good English. Frank put Charlie's arm around his neck, helped him into the shack, and seated him on the edge of the bunk. Charlie was young, his dark face broad out of all proportion to his slim body. There was a deep cut on his cheekbone plastered over with balsam gum, and one eye was swollen shut. He looked searchingly at Lute from one dark eye. Frank asked, "What was it?"

"I dunno, Frank. I met a strange team on Whitefish portage. I come up so quick on them I couldn't stop my dogs. Both teams was fightin', and this breed and me pulled 'em off. Then he turned on me and beat hell out of me."

"Why?"

"I dunno. He swung a trap in my face. When I fell, he kicked me. I heard him say somethin' about teaching me to stay out of his country. He broke my gun and pulled out."

"A breed, you say?" Frank said.

"Yes."

"You all right?"

"I got some busted ribs, I think."

Frank rose, and only then did he remember Lute. He introduced them. Charlie shook hands, not smiling. Lute's manner was faintly condescending.

Then Frank said, "I'm hitting the trail, Charlie. You take it easy."

He glanced up at Lute, and Lute stepped outside with him. Frank said, "The dogs will be

45

cut up, Lute. Have Charlie show you what to do. Tape his ribs too." He paused and added dryly, "You haven't got a white man's burden to carry with Charlie, Lute. He's been to school. Patronize him, and I hope he shoots you."

He didn't wait for Lute's answer. He put his head in the door and said, "Was he heading across Pembina, Charlie?" and when he got Charlie's nod, he grinned and said, "So long, kid."

He checked his load. Gun, a kettle, a slab of bannock and some tea, an ax, dog feed, bedroll, and that was all. He broke the sled loose, spoke quietly to the dogs, hewed them in behind Charlie's sled, and vanished into the night up Charlie's trail, heading west up the valley.

He traveled all that night, boiling tea twice and resting his dogs. He left Christmas Creek at the head of the valley, took Charlie's trail through two muskegs and over four ascending ridges, crossed the Wailing, which was now only a stream, and plunged into the long grade of tamarack scrub that put him on Whitefish before dawn. Just as light broke he came to where Charlie and the breed had fought on the short portage between Whitefish and Pembina Lakes. Charlie had left here yesterday noon. The breed, heading across Pembina, had trail to break. He would be starting about now, and that put him a half day ahead of Frank. With the breed's freshly broken trail to travel, it was a matter of a day to catch him.

The sky had cleared in the night, and morning

dawned with an iron cold. He was impatient to get on, but he fought it down. His dogs needed rest. Unhooking them, he fed them lightly, then built a fire and hunkered down beside it, gnawing on a piece of bannock, scooping up snow in his mittened hand to wash it down. The act recalled Kelcy McIvor and the strychnine on his old mittens. All this night the memory of her had been in the back of his mind, slowly building an anger and suspicion that he pondered now. Until his meeting with her, nobody had ever bothered to investigate his camp on Christmas Creek. Somehow, this girl, through a careless word, perhaps, had whetted someone's curiosity about him. Or maybe the word wasn't so careless; maybe it was her way of fighting him. And only the breed's carelessness or haste had made him overlook the tunnel. Frank shivered when he thought of it.

Before the hour he had promised himself was up, his impatience had conquered. He hooked up the dogs and started. It was a dazzling spotless world that he met that morning on the lake, and it lay dead and immobile in the grip of the cold. Plumes of frost hovered over the dogs, tipping each hair with silver, and the sled squealed on the dry snow. The trail crossed the arm of the Pembina, hugged the east shore for three miles, then turned into the bush. It held to an easterly direction, traveling the bare ridges. Frank hoped to come upon evidence that the man had stopped to kill some game for dog feed, which would bring their meeting sooner, but he did not. Before

47

noon he came to the man's night camp. After that, the trail was softer and slower. And through the afternoon to lowering dark, he dogged the man's trail. At early dark he had still not overtaken him. The breed might have feared pursuit, but Frank doubted it. Coming to a decision, he unhooked his dogs in the cold darkness, chained them out, fed them, and then took his gun and set off alone on the frozen trail, certain that his man couldn't be far ahead.

The trail was clinging to the crest of a jack-pine ridge, and in that utter darkness Frank followed it by feel. He was hungry and tired and was feeling the cold now, and the stars looked near and brittle as glass.

Soon, a mile from where he left the dogs, the trail tipped down into a creek. And then, once there, he saw the light of the man's fire several hundred yards ahead. He watched it a moment, considering. He tested the wind, and there was a faint stirring of it up the creek. If he approached from this side, the dogs would catch the scent and warn the breed.

Frank retreated up the ridge and made a wide half-mile circle that brought him to the creek above the fire. Screened now by the thickets of alders and willows, and with the deep snow to muffle his footsteps, he made his way down the creek. And then, fifty yards or so from the fire, the creek took a turn and he was looking at the camp. The breed had a roaring fire, and Frank noted carefully that some of his fuel was a jack pine, which snapped and crackled and made the night alive with sound. That would cover the noise of his approach. On three long poles rammed slanting into the snow, a tarp was stretched paralleling the fire. The breed sat on a spruce-bough bed in the heat reflected from the tarp, his cap and parka off, head bent over some task. Gently, Frank approached, rifle in hand.

Coming closer, he saw that the breed was repairing a snowshoe with babiche, or rawhide, which he was softening in the remains of his tea. His dogs were tied out behind the trap, and they were curled up now, nose in tail, fur ruffled for insulation against the night's cold, sleeping.

Calmly Frank walked on toward the fire, gun slacked off his shoulder. Suddenly, without looking up, the breed made a grab for a gun. Frank shot over his head. The dogs boiled out of their beds and set up a savage clamor, but they were chained and safe.

The warning shot stopped the breed. He stood up now, a thick and stocky man, and Frank walked into the circle of firelight. The breed cursed the dogs into silence, then faced Frank with a sullen, secretive expression.

Frank said mildly, "Jumpy, fella?"

The breed didn't answer, and Frank came closer to the fire, his rifle pointed at the breed. He kicked the man's rifle out into the snow, and then stood by his ax. "Sit down," he ordered.

The breed did. Frank squatted on the edge of the spruce boughs that the breed had cut for his bed and shoved his cap back off his forehead. His green eyes were glinting with sharp reflections of the fire, and he felt its warmth seeping into his tired muscles.

"I been on the trail a long time," Frank drawled. "I miss the company. Tell me a story."

Still the breed didn't answer. Frank said in a low hard voice, "You turned my shack upside down. Why?"

"I was out of grub," the breed said sullenly.

"You're a liar. I followed you out from Lobstick."

The breed said nothing.

"You tied into my partner yesterday. That because you were out of grub too?"

"He tried to kill my dogs."

"So you hit him in the face with a trap."

"That's a lie! He fell on a windfall!"

Frank said curiously, "Who sent you up this way?"

"It's my trap line," the breed answered. "I've trapped the Wailing for ten years."

"Do you always start trapping in the middle of the winter?" Frank drawled.

The breed shrugged, his dark eyes quiet and watchful.

Frank regarded him thoughtfully for a moment, and he could see the quiet sneering confidence in the man. It angered him, and puzzled him too. The breed had hung his traps, rifled his shack, beaten up Charlie, and now seemed doubtful if anything would happen to him.

Frank came to his feet. "Go over and haul your sled over here and throw it on the fire," he ordered crisply.

The breed's face changed, but he did not move. Frank swung his rifle up, levered a fresh shell into it, and waited. Slowly the breed came to his feet. "What you goin' to do?"

"I'm goin' to burn your sled and your harness and your grub," Frank said slowly. "That's the only kind of talk you understand."

There was fear in the breed's eyes now, but he didn't move. Frank said softly, "Hurry it up."

The breed walked around the fire to the sled, which was turned upside down. He righted it, sullenly threw the harness in it, then lifted its nose around till it pointed to the fire and dragged it over.

He paused with the sled's nose on a burning log, and went around to the handle bars as if to lift it on the fire. Instead, he shoved viciously. Propped up by the log, the sled drove across the fire into Frank's side, and the weight of it knocked him down. The breed leaped through the fire and landed atop him, driving the wind from him.

The breed slugged wildly at his face, and Frank brought his arms up in protection, dropping the gun. This was what the breed had been counting on. He rolled off Frank, lunging for the gun. Frank came over on his side, grabbed the breed by the shoulder, and held him, and with the other hand reached for the gun. They lay there side

51

by side, fighting to reach it, the breed kicking wildly.

Suddenly, Frank let go. The breed reached the rifle, and then Frank lunged on him. The breed heaved himself to his knees, Frank on his back, and swung the gun, butt foremost over his shoulder. It caught Frank in the neck and he was knocked backward. And then the breed heaved himself to his feet. Frank scrambled up, swinging savagely. His blow caught the breed flush behind the ear, and he staggered and fell. The gun slipped out of his hands into the snow and disappeared.

He came to his feet in time to meet Frank's rush. They stood there, knee deep in the snow, slugging wildly at each other, the breed grim and silent. The dogs were raising a bedlam of fury, straining at their chains, lips curled over teeth in a slavering fury.

Frank kept crowding the breed back, and then he beat the man's guard down and drove a smashing blow into his face that slipped on the man's teeth and tore his lip. The breed fell, and then reached for something in the snow. He came to his knees, a tamarack club in his hand. Frank went for him, and the breed swung the club. It caught Frank on the shoulder and sent him rolling into the snow at the feet of a dog.

He felt the dog slash at him, heard his parka hood rip, and then he saw the breed run for the fire and the ax. Frank rose and ran too, and left his feet in a long dive at the breed's back. They both landed in the middle of the roaring fire. Frank rolled away, and the breed, yelling with pain, clawed his way out of the fire to the pile of dry logs that he had dragged up for fuel. Some dogged instinct had made him keep the ax, and now he came to his feet on the uncertain footing of the logs.

Frank lunged at him, pinning his arms to his sides, and the impact of his rush took them over backward. Suddenly the breed screamed with pain, and they hit the snow.

The breed lay there, moaning, and Frank came off him, dragging in great shuddering breaths of the bitter air. And then Frank saw what had happened.

The breed's leg had become wedged down among the heavy logs, and when Frank slammed into him, carrying them both down, the breed's leg had broken.

Frank lifted off the log, then sank to his knees, exhausted, his head hung with weariness. Presently the breed's moans roused him, and he looked up. The man's leg was twisted awkwardly, and he moved his head from side to side with the pain.

Frank grasped him by the shoulders and dragged him over onto the spruce bed, then threw two logs on the fire. He was shaking with weariness, and hunger was gnawing at his belly. His face felt bloody and smashed. The dogs, silent now, were standing alertly, waiting for the next move of this strange drama.

The breed was quiet, but his bruised face was

53

gray with pain, and all the malevolence had gone out of his dark eyes.

He asked calmly, "You goin' to leave me now?"

"I ought to," Frank answered harshly.

"You can't do that," the breed said quietly.

Frank knelt by him, fighting down his pity. He said curtly, "It's time to talk, fella. Who sent you up to me?"

"Nobody. I just come," the man answered through clamped teeth. His eyes were stubborn, adamant, and Frank knew he wouldn't talk. For the breed was certain that Frank wouldn't desert him, wouldn't deny him help; it was a code that all men obeyed in this country, one that he would have obeyed himself. And knowing it, he wouldn't talk.

Frank came to his feet unsteadily. He was too weary to care whether the breed talked, or to derive much satisfaction out of the fact that he'd taught a snooper a lesson. It was an expensive lesson for them both, for he would have to take the man back to Lobstick.

With a dead weariness, Frank set about doing what he knew he would have to do. He split out two splints with the ax, then reached in his belt for his hunting knife. Somewhere in the brawl, it had slipped out of its sheath. The breed, watching him said, "Mine's over there," indicating the bedroll.

Frank went over to where the bedroll and grub box and duffel sack were. He picked up the duffel sack, and the breed said sharply, "It's a knife you want, ain't it? It's in the grub bag."

Frank looked up swiftly, suspicious at the urgency in the man's voice. Then he deliberately opened the drawstring of the duffel sack and dumped out its contents. Besides the change of moccasins and socks, the sewing kit, and the rolled babiche, there was something else there in a deer-hide sack. He picked it up and looked at the breed. The man's eyes were dark with hate.

Frank opened the sack and shook out a small bottle filled with white powder.

Slowly a thin smile broke Frank's gaunt, bruised face, and he picked up the bottle and came over to the breed.

"Nice stuff," he murmured. "It does a quick job, doesn't it?"

The breed didn't say anything.

"I'll keep this," Frank went on. "If you figure to horn in on my line again and loot my shack, you better think twice. Millis would like to see this strychnine. You get it?"

Still the breed didn't anwer. Frank pocketed the strychnine.

"Something else, too," he said quietly. "Tell your pals to stay away from me — clear away from me. If they don't you'll wind up outside behind bars — along with Bruce McIvor, the guy that sold it to you."

The breed nodded now; he understood.

Frank remembered Kelcy McIvor's words: "I'll make him destroy it — all of it." He wondered if she had even tried. And he wondered, too, at the courage of the girl. If she was seeking some evidence against him to cancel out his evidence against her brother, she was playing a tougher game than she knew. And she'd almost succeeded.

Chapter Four

It was a strange sight when Frank, more gaunt and black-bearded than ever, pulled into Lobstick five days later. The breed, in a high fever lay in the cariole, and two teams, eleven dogs in tandem, pulled him. It had been five days of hell — five days of breaking trail, of hunting dog feed each night because he couldn't carry it, and of stopping a half-dozen times a day to heat rocks so that the breed's leg would not freeze in the iron cold that gripped the land.

At dusk that afternoon he left the breed at Lobstick's hospital, which consisted of five beds on the glassed-in porch of the doctor's residence. His next move was to hunt up Millis. He found him at his office in the rear of his trim white and green house behind a picket fence on a back road of Lobstick. The lamp in Millis' office was lighted against the deepening dusk. When he answered Frank's knock, Frank stepped into a small room, benches lining two walls, a desk and chair in the center of the room, and a tiny single jail cell of four-by-four timbers in the rear corner opposite a stove.

Millis had been doing paperwork. He pulled off his reading glasses and shook hands with Frank and motioned him to a bench. Frank was weary to the bone, dead for sleep, but he knew he must take this insurance.

"I just left a breed with a broken leg over at the hospital," he said. "I thought you might want to know."

Millis' brown tunic fitted his shoulders trimly. Sitting there, he looked more benevolent than stern, yet his eyes, mild and watchful, missed nothing.

"Who was he?"

"Joe McKenzie. I broke his leg, I'm afraid."

Millis was politely silent. Frank told him of following the breed's trail up the Wailing, of discovering that his traps were jerked, of the house turned inside out, and of Charlie's brush with him. Frank framed his story cleverly, making it seem that his resentment stemmed from the fact that his traps were hung and his line was trespassed upon.

He finished, "I overtook him at night. I warned him off my line, and he got tough, claiming he'd trapped the Wailing for ten years. Has he?"

"No. Then what?"

"Words led to blows. We slugged it out until he took to his ax. I piled into him then, but his foot was jammed in some windfalls he'd dragged up for the fire. The fall broke his leg."

"And you brought him back?" Millis asked. Frank nodded.

Millis tilted back in his chair and said obliquely, carelessly, "That's too bad — too bad for you, too, Nearing."

"I don't see it."

"Don't get me wrong," Millis drawled. "I'm not blaming you for what you did. Chances are, Joe won't make a complaint, and I wouldn't listen to him if he did. He's slippery, and knows enough to stay away from me. I didn't mean it that way."

"How did you?"

Millis scrubbed his jaw with the palm of his hand and looked searchingly at Frank. "You know," he said, "we police mind our own business pretty well. We never ask questions. If a man is trying to forget his past and build on the future, we let him alone. But strangely enough, other people haven't got our tolerance."

Frank scowled, not understanding.

"You're a stranger here," Millis went on. "You've been here six months. Outside of myself, you haven't spoken to a soul, have you?"

"No."

Millis nodded. "That's what I mean. You're a secretive devil, Nearing. People don't like mysteries." He brought his chair down and put his elbows on the desk. "I'll bet money that Joe McKenzie did this to you out of curiosity."

"You think so?"

Millis nodded and smiled faintly. "Take a tip from me, while I'm not minding my own business. Be a little more friendly. You can have a drink with a man and still beat hell out of him if he crowds you." He paused and said then, "You know, people are beginning to think you're inventing a death ray or something up in Christmas Valley."

Frank forced a smile. "All I'm trying to invent is money enough out of my winter and spring hunt to grub-stake me for a prospect next summer."

"Tell 'em that," Millis said. "That's all they want to know."

Frank rose and said, "Thanks, Millis. Am I clear?"

"Seem to be. I'll get Joe's story tonight. If it doesn't jibe with yours, I think I'll take your version. You can leave his dogs here."

They shook hands and Frank went out. Even Millis was curious about him now, he thought in deep disgust. He unhooked the breed's dogs and chained them out, then headed for the hotel. So Millis thought there was such a thing as being too solitary? He had framed it in the way of friendly advice, but underneath it was a disapproval and a watchfulness that Frank didn't like.

His dogs put up and fed, Frank went to the barbershop, got a shave and a bath, and came out into the dark street. He turned, almost unconsciously, toward McIvor's big post at the head of the street, determined to satisfy the persistent nagging of the curiosity that had been with him these last five days.

The big radio on the dry-goods counters was booming, and the people around it eyed Frank in a kind of trancelike silence, listening to the Korean war news, as he walked to the counter on the opposite side. He had seen Kelcy McIvor, arms folded on the counter, listening. She straightened now and crossed the store to him. She was wearing a green sweater and skirt today, and Frank noted thankfully that she was not wearing boots, and also that her ankles were trim. She came up behind the counter and paused there and said, "Something for you?" in a manner reminiscent of stores that make a point of cowing customers. She was not very happy to see him.

Frank almost smiled and gibed gently, "Yes, I'd like to see some of your chartreuse underwear — a two-pants suit."

Kelcy said quickly, "We've nothing in chartreuse, but we have a little hair number in peach that I'm sure you'd like. Won't you step outside and try it on?"

Frank did smile then; it was the ghost of a smile, and it was in acknowledgment of her temper that he was sure would not fail her. Kelcy didn't smile, and there was plain unfriendliness in her eyes.

Frank put a leg up on the counter and sat down, and said quietly, "I didn't know if you'd remember me."

"Perfectly. It was such a charming afternoon."

"You remember that?" Frank asked softly. "Somehow, I thought you'd forgotten it."

Kelcy caught the undertone of something close to threat in his voice. She said, "Blackmail isn't easy to forget."

"Not for me, but I wondered if it was for you."

"What do you mean by that?"

Frank drew his hand from his parka pocket.

With his body screening that hand from the radio listeners across the room, he set the fat little bottle of strychnine on the counter. He did not look at it; he watched Kelcy's face. She smothered a start of surprise and looked up quickly at him. He put the bottle back in his pocket.

Kelcy looked across the room, then said, "Come back where we can talk."

Frank followed her into a storeroom in the rear. She shut the door and kneed an almost empty keg of nails across to block it, then turned to him. The lamp in the wall bracket was turned down; Frank turned it up and confronted her.

"Where did you get that?" Kelcy asked.

"From a curious man," Frank murmured. "Remember, you told me everybody was curious about me?"

"But where?"

"He'd rifled my shack. I followed him and we —"

"I've heard about it already. It's Joe McKenzie."

Frank nodded. "I took this from his outfit."

Kelcy looked searchingly at Frank. "And why did you come to me about it?"

Frank answered dryly, "I haven't tasted the stuff, but I think it's part of what your brother brought in."

"That's a lie," Kelcy said calmly.

Frank shrugged. "Maybe. Still, the blackmail that worked on you will work on Joe McKenzie, I think." He hefted the bottle in his hand and said, "Joe didn't deny he got it from Bruce McIvor."

"But he couldn't have! Bruce had five ten-ounce bottles. I disposed of them."

"The package I picked up weighed at least five pounds," Frank murmured.

In the following silence, Kelcy regarded him cautiously and with a new curiosity. She said slowly, reluctantly, "Now you have me worried."

"That's what I want."

Kelcy leaned against the door and folded her arms across her breast. "May I have that to show Bruce?"

"No."

"Why not?"

Again Frank hefted the bottle, then slipped it in the pocket of his parka. His deeply tanned face looked gaunt and fanatic in the uncertain lamplight. "I didn't come here to discipline your kid brother," he said crisply. "You've missed the point. We made a bargain that day in the hotel."

"It was more a threat, wasn't it — if you turn in Bruce, I'll set Millis on you?"

Frank nodded. "You haven't put Millis on me, but you put Joe McKenzie. There's not much choice between the two. I don't like it."

"You're mistaken," Kelcy said quietly.

"I could be. Still, until our talk at the hotel, I was left alone. Afterward, my shack was searched."

"What have you got out there, a gold mine?" Kelcy asked drily.

"I'm working on a magnetic ray," Frank said, irony in his voice. "When I get it perfected, I can draw the moon down to the Eiffel Tower. I'll climb aboard then with some bees and some grapes and raise vine leaves for my hair."

Kelcy smiled tentatively, without much humor. "I'd be the last person to stop you from doing that."

"Then keep your pals from breathing down my neck," Frank said shortly.

Kelcy straightened up. "There's not much sense in this talk," she said, an edge to her voice. "I'm not faintly interested in you or what you're doing. I never was. I was forced into taking an interest because you were a threat to Bruce."

"I still am."

"I tell you, I had nothing to do with Joe McKenzie!" Kelcy flared.

Frank hunched his shoulders. "One more strike and you're out," he said. "That's a promise." He started for the door.

The conversation was finished. Frank kicked the nail keg away from the door while Kelcy watched him, anger stirring in her blue eyes. She said then, "Either you're a squaw man and you're ashamed of it, or you're an embezzler in hiding, or you're just a ham Thoreau up on your Walden Pond! Whatever you are, I'll leave you alone and I'll see that Bruce leaves you alone. So the next man that comes up there out of grub and asking for some, you can shoot him without referring it to me."

Frank said gravely, "Thanks just oodles," and went out.

Kelcy stared at his broad back as he walked the length of the store. She hated him, and she didn't understand him. What was the matter with the man? Maybe he was like the Englishman her father told her about who hated people so much that he built a shack on the edge of the Barrens and lived like a beast rather than associate with them. But this man had a partner — two partners, an Indian and the big suspicious blond man. It wasn't solitude he wanted; it was to be let completely and utterly alone.

Kelcy closed the storeroom door, so angry her hands were shaking. She took a deep breath and got a sort of control over herself. She saw Frank step out into the cold night, a plume of steam sweeping across the floor as he opened the door. There was a kind of hostile loneliness about that scene that stirred her, and then vanished. There was no misunderstanding his threat.

The store was empty when Bruce came in at seven. Kelcy heard him shut the rear door and she went back to meet him, a haste driving her. Bruce was hanging up his hat and coat in the storeroom; he said, "I'll take over, Sis."

"Not until you answer for a few things," Kelcy said grimly.

Bruce looked sharply at her. His dark face, pleasant and weak, was set in a defensive scowl. "Now what?"

"Frank Nearing was in here just now. You

heard about his tangle with Joe McKenzie?"

"I heard," Bruce answered in a neutral wary voice.

"After Nearing beat him up, he found a bottle of strychnine in his outfit, Bruce."

"So what?" Bruce asked defiantly.

As Kelcy watched him, she knew in her heart that what Frank Nearing had suspected was true. Bruce couldn't hide anything from her, and his guilt was on his weak face even before the accusation.

She sat down on a coil of rope and leaned back against the wall. "Bruce, why are you such a fool?" she asked bitterly.

"What are you talking about?"

Kelcy made a weary gesture. "It's no use lying. You gave me five ten-ounce bottles and told me that was all. You lied. You brought in five pounds. And you sold the rest, I suppose."

Bruce didn't answer. He watched his sister with a kind of breathless wariness, waiting to hear the rest.

Kelcy was finished. She got up, took her coat and hat from the nail, and slipped her feet into galoshes. She started for the door. Bruce said, "Wait, Sis!"

Kelcy turned, waiting for what he had to say.

"What are you going to do?"

"Nothing," Kelcy said softly. "Frank Nearing will do it for me. He said he wouldn't report it this time. But one more strike and you're out, Bruce. Those were his words."

"What does he care?" Bruce said hotly. "I'm not hurting him!"

Kelcy was about to answer, and then thought better of it. "He does care," she said steadily, "and that's what you ought to worry about."

"Nobody's using it up in his country!" Kelcy didn't bother to answer, and Bruce added bitterly, "That pious bush tramp! I'd like to break his neck!"

"I wouldn't advise trying it," Kelcy said calmly, and added with a friendly bluntness, "There's a man who isn't impressed by your charm, Bruce. He's warned you. And you'd better wipe your nose, or you're going to get in real trouble."

Bruce glared at her.

Kelcy said, turning to the door, "I hope I don't see Dad's face when you come to the pay-off."

"Shut up!"

"O.K. Have it your own way."

Kelcy went out, and Bruce stared at the door a long while after it was closed. Reluctantly, almost, he set about building the fire in the storeroom stove, a precaution against the stored canned goods freezing during the bitter night. That done, he walked moodily toward the front of the store, his trim shoulders hunched, hands thrust in the front pockets of his breeches, dark face saturnine and sulking. He leaned his shoulder against the back counter, put his foot up on a front counter shelf, and stared moodily at the vacant store. He wasn't afraid of Kelcy's telling on him; she was too loyal. It was Frank Nearing he had to fear

— Frank and Saul both. Right now, he was shouldering all the risk in this, with Saul covering up for himself. If Nearing spilled it, Saul would be clear.

He thought of Saul, rather than Frank, wondering about him — and about Bonnie. It was queer, those two living there in the hotel a room apart from each other. For one bleak moment he wondered about Bonnie, and then he wouldn't think about it. Bonnie had told him it was all right, that Saul was only a business friend and that she was able to take care of herself. She loved him, and God knows he loved her. Bonnie was straight. Every time she smiled at him, something seemed to melt inside him, but she was straight. All the same, he was uneasy, and turned his thoughts to Nearing, trying to recall all he'd heard of him. The sum total was nothing. Bruce hated him suddenly with the hot and unreasoning hatred of all men for a righteous man who might be a squealer.

His reverie was interrupted by the opening of the front door. A woman stepped in and headed for the post-office wicket; before the door closed, Bonnie came through too.

At sight of her, Bruce waved and smiled, then went in behind the wicket.

"I want Gus Nelson's mail," the woman said.

Bruce reached up to the N pigeonhole, sorted the letters, and gave her only a T. Eaton's Co. advertising circular. She left, and Bonnie stepped to the window.

"Stealing stamps?" she asked, smiling.

But Bruce only grinned and did not look up. He was looking through the letters in his hand, a musing expression on his face, and he stopped at one, a long official envelope, and laid it aside.

Bonnie screwed her head around and read, "Frank Nearing." She looked up at Bruce, and Bruce said, "What's his partner's name?"

"Westock, isn't it? Why?"

Bruce drew another sheaf of mail down from the W section, searched it, and brought out a lone letter. By that time there was alarm in Bonnie's face.

"What are you doing, Bruce?"

Bruce seemed undecided for a moment, then he took the letters and left the wicket. "Come on back," he said to Bonnie.

Bonnie silently followed him back to the warm storeroom. On his way, Bruce took down a small teakettle from the nest of them hanging on a bale overhead. He went into the rear of the storeroom, put a cup of water in the kettle at the sink pump, and put the kettle on the stove. Then he passed Bonnie and closed the door.

Again Bonnie asked, "What are you going to do, Bruce?"

Bruce only grinned and came up and put his arms around her. Bonnie kissed him dutifully, gave him a fleeting smile, and then said with soft alarm, "Better put them back, kid."

"What?"

"Those letters."

"It's easy," Bruce said, grinning. "Besides, I'm curious."

Bonnie said sharply, "Don't be a fool, Bruce! You aren't going to open them, are you?"

"Why not? I've done it before."

"But what'll it get you — outside of a stretch in prison?"

Bruce said grimly, "Nearing is riding hell out of me. I'm going to find out why he's here, and what about him. I tell you, I'm curious."

Bonnie gripped his arm. "But you can't do it, Bruce! It's the same as mail robbery, and they give you ten years for that!"

"Who'll know, unless you tell them?"

"That's not the point! It's the risk!"

"It's my risk."

"It's not!" Bonnie said passionately. "What if they make you tell why you did it! Nearing will tell them. And then you'll drag us in!"

"Us?" Bruce's voice had a little edge to it.

"Yes, me and Saul," Bonnie said defiantly.

"Oh, so it's Saul you're worrying about?"

"Don't be like that!" Bonnie cried. "I'm only telling you what will happen!"

Bruce said thinly, "You seem damned concerned about Saul, Bonnie. Why?"

"I'm worried about myself — and you. Can't you see that?"

Bruce's voice was ugly. "I'm not so sure. You're worried about Saul. Bonnie, are you two-timing me?"

"Oh, damn!" Bonnie said, in complete exasperation. "Are you going to start that again, Bruce? I don't give a hoot about Saul, except that he's put up money for my restaurant! All I'm trying to tell you is that we're running enough risks, without mail robbery added to it!"

Bruce looked at her in bleak silence, his eyes hot and suspicious and afraid and pleading. Bonnie had seen that look before. She came over and took Bruce's head in her hands and kissed him, and then looked up at him. "You jealous, simple fool," she murmured.

Bruce said thickly, "Bonnie, if you're lyin' to me I'll kill you, so help me!"

"If I'm lying, I hope you do."

There was a moment of silence, and then Bonnie said softly, "Bruce, put those letters back. Please. For me."

"No," Bruce said stubbornly. "I've done it before. There's no risk to it, and you can't tell they've been opened." He burst out passionately, "Let me alone, won't you, Bonnie? I know what I'm doing!"

There was a rash and wild look in his face and Bonnie knew it was useless to argue. If he was crossed, he got ugly and stubborn and headstrong, and his temper was a wild thing that she couldn't brook.

She sighed resignedly. "All right. Only hurry. I'll watch the front. Lock that back door and hurry it."

They had a few moments to wait until the water boiled, and it was spent in strained silence. Fi-

71

nally, the kettle began to sing, and Bruce went about steaming the letters open. He read them both, while Bonnie watched the front of the store. She heard him go dump the water into the sink and turned around to watch him.

"Don't tell me about it," she said swiftly. "I don't want anything to do with it, not anything." She put her hands over her ears.

Bruce was smiling. "I think I'll go on a little trip tomorrow, Bonnie. Up the Wailing. I'm the mailman."

Bonnie only shook her head and went out into the store, feeling a vast relief. The lawless unbridled temper of him made her afraid. She remembered that look in his eye when he promised to kill her if she was unfaithful to him, and she shivered a little. She knew he would do it, too, if he ever learned what she and Saul were to each other.

Chapter Five

Three miles below the entrance of Whitefish Creek into the Wailing, Charlie Cree had cut a trail to the west that presently opened onto Swan Lake. Charlie's trail skirted the south shore, vanished into a stand of birch at the foot of a bay, threaded a tortuous muskeg, and opened into a broken, uncertain country where Charlie had once seen marten tracks. It swung north finally and entered Christmas Valley at its southwest corner. Charlie had never caught a marten there, stone or pine, but he religiously made the rounds of this line, taking two days at it, usually returning with a moose or a deer he had killed.

When Frank came to that fresh trail at cold and brittle noon on his way home, he tested it and swung his dogs into it, glad of the news it told him. For it was fresh, and Charlie must be up and around and his dogs fit again.

An hour's run over a good trail brought Frank out onto the lake. Here the trail left the shore and cut across the mile of sun-dazzled snow on the open lake to the far shore. He followed it with curiosity, wondering what Charlie was up to. Nearing the farther shore, he saw two men and a dog team on the lake just off a poplar point, and they were fiddling with something.

When he came closer, Charlie and Lute stood up to greet him.

Frank whoaed his dogs and looked at the scene. A bull moose had broken through the ice here just off a point of land, and he was dead. Charlie had a noose around his head, and had hitched the dogs to a rope that trailed out ahead to give both himself and Lute a purchase in dragging the big fellow out of the hole.

All that was dropped now at Frank's approach. He shook hands all around, and they broke out smokes, sitting on the sleds. Lute's face was flushed with exertion, and he was smiling with pleasure now as Frank offered him his tobacco pouch and he rolled a cigarette. Charlie, not talking, already knew that Frank was satisfied by his trip. He was quiet, taciturn, Frank saw.

"Well, who was the mystery man, and where'd you come from?" Lute asked, sitting on the nose of Frank's sled. Charlie squatted in the snow, pinching his cigarette in his long brown fingers.

Frank told of the chase, of the fight, of his visit to Lobstick, and finally of his conversation with Kelcy McIvor. Charlie only grunted.

"So it's that brat of a brother again?" Lute mused, when Frank was finished. "What did the girl say this time?"

"She didn't say," Frank murmured. "She didn't have to. I have the evidence this trip." He drew out the corked bottle of strychnine, and Lute and Charlie looked at it and gave it back gingerly, as if it might explode.

Then Lute said, "Any mail for me, Frank?"

"None for anybody," Frank said. Lute swore in disgust. Frank caught Charlie's glance, a little worried, and shrugged. In this mail they had both expected that Frank would get a letter from the recording office at Fort Resource, confirming the rules for the forfeiture of a claim. In a legal fight that might ensue, this would be valuable evidence.

Frank talked to Charlie then, asked about his ribs, saw that the deep cut on Charlie's face was healing well, and then turned to their business.

"What happened here?" Frank asked, walking over to look at the moose.

Charlie grinned at last, his old grin. "I was just leaving the lake for the portage across the point into those birch," he said. "I jumped him feeding out here on the point. He took one step off the point and went through."

"Sulphur spring?" Frank asked.

Charlie nodded. "He couldn't get back because the bank was too steep, and he couldn't quite make it up on the good ice when he got through the rotten stuff. I shot him, and figured to windlass him up on the bank, but there wasn't a tree big enough to take his weight. I went back for him." He nodded toward Lute.

The gesture was eloquent of Charlie's opinion of Lute, and Frank knew immediately that Charlie didn't like him either. A week together had told Charlie all he wanted to know about their new partner, and he had made up his mind. Frank guessed that Lute was the reason Charlie had hit the trail again, alone. He wanted to be away from Lute. The man's quiet gall, his alert curiosity would earn him no affection from Charlie. And in a negative way, it explained to Frank why Lute was so glad to see him. Charlie could clam up when he didn't like a man, and Lute had suffered too. He was hungry for talk, and right now he was torn between that hunger and pride. He stood at Frank's elbow, silently regarding the moose after his first talkative outburst.

Frank felt a kind of pity toward him. "Ever eat brisket, Lute?"

"Can't say I have."

"Get a pot boiling up in the brush and we'll have a feed."

Lute left to build the fire, while Charlie and Frank unhooked Frank's dogs and put them ahead of Charlie's team. Charlie didn't talk much and finally Frank, impatient, growled, "Why don't you say it, Charlie?"

Charlie looked up. "You got his money?"

"Half of it."

"Then it's all right," Charlie said calmly.

"You have any trouble with him?"

Charlie looked at him a long time, then shook his head.

Frank jibed fondly, "Go ahead. Tell me your old man had a word for him. Your old man would have said, 'Big white man speaks with forked tongue.'"

Charlie laughed then, and nodded. "That's

about it, Frank. Only he would have made med- icine against him."

Frank suddenly felt a hot loyalty for Charlie. What was necessary, Charlie would suffer; and Lute and his money were necessary. Charlie didn't question it.

They called Lute over then. Charlie, with a long spruce pole, got a pry on the moose, and Lute and Frank, with Charlie cursing the two dog teams into action, succeeded in skidding the moose out onto the good ice. Frank and Charlie worked swiftly, for the water would quickly freeze on the hide. They skinned him out, set the brisket to boiling, then leisurely finished the job of butch- ering. It was dark by the time the job was done and the meat cut up so that they could carry it. They and the dogs feasted that night.

Next day, Lute broke trail on ahead, while Charlie and Frank, their sleds loaded heavily with meat and their dogs lazy from glutting, finished the circle of Charlie's marten line and slipped down into Christmas Valley after dark that after- noon.

Nearing the shack, Frank, first behind Lute, noticed his dogs suddenly lift their tired heads and keen the air. A moment later, snaking through the thick stand of spruce, he came upon Lute, motionless, at the edge of the clearing.

Lute called back in a low voice, "There's a light in camp, Frank."

"Go on," Frank said curtly.

They moved on toward the shack, and now

in the clear Frank could see that a lamp was lighted in the shack, and smoke was lifting to the canyon rim in the still air.

He stopped his dogs by the cache, and Charlie came up behind him. Then the three of them made hurriedly for the door.

Frank was the first to enter, and he hauled up just inside the door. There, sitting at the table, chair tilted back, a half-smile on his dark face, sat Bruce McIvor.

"Gentlemen," he said mockingly.

Lute and Charlie entered and shut the door. Frank regarded Bruce with a puzzled suspicion that narrowed his eyes for a moment.

Then he said quietly, "Did you come up to get it straight from the horse's mouth, McIvor?"

"Call it that if you want," Bruce drawled.

Frank turned to Charlie. "This is the joker that was peddling the strychnine, Charlie."

Bruce only smiled and didn't say anything.

"Make yourself at home," Frank murmured. "We've got work to do. I'll talk to you later. Lute, you entertain him." The light of a sudden wry humor flickered in Frank's eyes. He drew the bottle of strychnine from his parka pocket and stepped beyond the table and set the bottle where Bruce could see it on the edge of a rough shelf holding several books. He said to Lute, not looking at Bruce, "Tell him a story, Lute. Tell him the one about the little bottle of white powder and the policeman. It's a favorite of his, because he thinks it's a fairy story."

Bruce smiled faintly and Frank and Charlie stepped out into the night. They both moved in the same direction, toward the drifted trail that led to the tunnel entrance. Charlie squatted and tested the edge of a track. The snow crumbled immediately under little pressure. He said quietly, "He's had a look at it, Frank. There are his tracks."

Frank said slowly, "Maybe it's time to throw a scare into him that'll make him forget it."

They unloaded the sled, unhooked the dogs, fed them, and fed Bruce's team, which was chained out in the timber behind the shack.

Afterward they came in. Frank pulled off his parka, and Charlie settled onto the edge of the bunk. Bruce hadn't changed his seat, and Lute now came away from the stove, his eyes alert and watchful.

Frank kicked a stool up to the table and sat down. "Now," he began, "let's hear your beef."

"Beef?" Bruce inquired. "What have I got to beef about?"

"Your sister said you didn't like the bush. You've spent a couple of days in it to reach me. You must want something."

Bruce slowly reached inside his windbreaker and brought out two crumpled letters. "I just thought I'd bring you your mail," he said. "There's one for each of you."

Lute came over and picked his letter up. Frank reached over for his. Lute turned his over, and then looked quickly at Bruce.

"This has been opened!" Lute said sharply.

"So has the other," Bruce said. He smiled faintly.

Frank drew out his letter. It was from the recording office. It stated the rules for the forfeiture of a claim, and the requirements for the granting of a patent. He stared at it a long time, not even reading it, and let the significance sink into his mind. Bruce McIvor had opened the letters. He now knew, couldn't help but know, that Frank was getting ready to restake a claim that had been forfeited. And everyone in Lobstick knew of the old Christmas Creek claim. Putting this letter and the new door in the tunnel together, adding Frank's secrecy and his resentment against visitors, Bruce McIvor knew the whole secret that Frank had fought to keep these many months.

Frank folded the letter and glanced up at Lute. Lute had just finished reading his letter, and his face was ugly with anger. Bruce McIvor had a cigarette in the corner of his mouth and was rubbing the head of a match, watching Frank.

It was Lute who first moved. He drove a fist into Bruce's face with a power that knocked him clean off the stool and against the wall.

Frank lunged to his feet and leaped on Lute's back, pinning his arms behind him. Lute, cursing wildly, fought to get free, kicking out at Bruce.

Frank wheeled him around and pushed him away, and Lute turned, his face savage with anger.

"Cut it!" Frank said sharply. He was between Lute and Bruce, whom Charlie had hauled to his feet by the collar of his shirt.

"Let me at him!" Lute raged. "I'll kill him!"

"You'll sit down and shut up," Frank said softly, "or I'll have to show you again that I'm running this outfit."

He turned to Bruce McIvor, who was rubbing his jaw. His dark eyes were wicked with anger and with fear. It was easy to see that he had not counted on this, and he seemed a little puzzled, as if he were trying to recall what it was in Lute's letter that justified this anger.

"Sit down," Frank said curtly.

Charlie shoved Bruce onto the stool, and then Frank put a leg on the stool opposite.

"You better talk, and talk plain," Frank said bluntly. "How'd you get hold of these letters?"

"My dad's the postmaster," Bruce said sullenly.

"Why'd you open them?"

"You know damn well why I opened them!" Bruce sneered. "Sis told me what you told her! I took a chance on steaming open your letter, and when I found out what was in it I didn't bother to seal it up again. I've got you now, Nearing! You aren't going blabbing to Millis about me now!"

He shifted his glance to Lute. "When I get to a newspaper I can find out why you're hiding out too, Westock."

Frank said calmly, "Just what do you know about me?"

Bruce laughed. "I know you've found ore on this claim. It isn't yours, either, and you're writing

81

to check on the forfeiture rules. I also figured out that old Christiansen quit workin' on this claim about three years ago, too, so you haven't got long to wait to restake."

Frank eyed him gravely. "And now you know, what will you do?"

Bruce leaned forward. "You know damn well what I'll do, Nearing! You know about this strychnine. Well, it's a pretty nice thing for me, and I'm not going to have you sticking your puss in it and gumming up the works! You won't now, either." He laughed. "Another thing you won't do, in case you're afraid. You won't put me out of the way. I figured about that a long time, and I know you're afraid to. You aren't the kind of bush tramp that would kill a man — you're educated!"

He glared triumphantly at Frank and then at Lute, and leaned back in his chair. "Now that you've got all the steam worked off and are willing to listen, I'll make my deal. That's what I came here for."

Frank looked over at Charlie, whose face was impassive. Charlie shrugged faintly. Lute was standing there, an expression of alert interest in his small face.

Frank said, "What's the deal?"

"Shut up about me, and I'll shut up about you and this strike. I'll forget I saw the letters."

"And if I won't make the deal?"

"I'll spread the word around about what's going on here. I'll get hold of Christiansen and tell him, and he'll spoil your plans for you." He looked at Lute. "I'll tell Millis about your letter, too. He might be interested to know that Carl says the search is clear off the trail, and that you seem safe enough where you are."

Lute smiled crookedly. He now had perfect control of himself. "Boo," he said mockingly.

Bruce pointed out shrewdly, "But you were worried enough about it to slug me."

"That was for opening my mail. I'd slug you if I'd found you'd opened a tailor's bill addressed to me."

Bruce laughed nastily. His confidence had returned, and he knew he had the upper hand now. He said to Frank, "There's something else I want, too, Nearing. I'll take a piece of this strike of yours, just to sweeten things up. It'll be signed and witnessed by these two."

Frank said thinly, "Maybe you're wrong about my being — educated."

But Bruce McIvor only laughed. He shook his head and said, "That's the deal. Take it or leave it."

Frank looked at Charlie and nodded toward the door. Frank stepped outside then, and Charlie followed him.

Out in the raw cold, Frank faced Charlie. "How does it look?"

"He's no good," Charlie said quietly. "He couldn't keep a secret, Frank. Not even if he made money out of it."

"He's a rummy," Frank said bitterly. "He'd

get tanked in Lobstick and talk, and the whole town would move up here to stake this out." Frank groaned then, and smashed his fist into his palm. "Three weeks, Charlie — three damned weeks — and I don't care who he tells! Our claim will be recorded then!"

"Can you hold him here?"

"And have a search party with Millis heading it come up here and find him?"

"What else?"

The door opened and Lute stepped out then.

"Well, that tears it for you," he said gloomily. "Are you going to take him up?"

"What was in your letter?" Frank asked, not even apologizing for asking it.

"It was from my lawyer. My wife's got the law on me, just as I thought she would." He added grimly, "I'd like to twist that kid's head off. I don't like people snooping in my mail."

Frank grunted. "Well, you're on the spot, too, fella. Any suggestions?"

Lute hesitated for a moment, as if about to say something, and then changed his mind. He said quietly, "There's no choice. Better take him up."

Frank was quiet a long moment. He stood there in the night, shivering, and he suddenly knew that he was not going to lose this without a fight. A summer of misery, of sacrifice, of hopes held in check, of luck, of grinding labor, of risk, and of nerves wire thin with anxiety — all of it was suffered so that a worthless, dishonest cub would profit by it. It wasn't going to happen.

Frank said quietly, "Let's eat. I'll think about it."

They went in, and Charlie and Frank set about getting something to eat. Bruce McIvor smoked and kept his silence.

They ate moose steaks and biscuits, nobody talking, and afterward lighted smokes. When Bruce McIvor could stand it no longer, he said, "Well, is it a deal, Nearing?"

Frank didn't answer. He got up and went over to a bunk and took down a canvas packsack. He said to Charlie, "That will hold two bannocks, one blanket, some tea, some sugar, matches, a kettle, a box of shells, a knife, and some salt, Charlie. Help me round the stuff up, will you?"

Wordlessly, Charlie cleared off the table, and he and Frank got together the things he named. Bruce McIvor watched them with a jeering contempt in his eyes that slowly gave way to anxiety.

When all the stuff was assembled on the table, Frank said to Bruce, "Need anything more? A change of socks, maybe?"

"What for?"

Frank sat down and brought out his pouch and rolled a cigarette carefully. "You're right about this claim, McIvor. In three weeks it will automatically be forfeit and I'll stake it, with just a few changes. But you won't be anywhere near a mail plane or a radio or a telegraph to stop me."

"No?" Bruce said, suddenly cautious.

"No. Tomorrow, Charlie and you and I are starting out on a trip. It's five hard days' travel with dogs back to the height of land. On the other side you can pick up a creek that empties into Horn Lake. You can follow that out till you come to a portage on Horn Lake. There's a trader there — Weymarn. He does a little trapping in the winter over across Horn Lake to some of those outfits at the edge of the Barren Land." He paused, watching Bruce McIvor's dark face. "It takes three days' hard travel on shoes to make Weymarn's crossing from the height of land. It'll take six days' hard travel on shoes to make it back here. Your sister says you're no bushman. I think you'll head for Weymarn's unless you want to starve, because I'll give you only two days' grub and no gun. Weymarn usually makes a trip in late winter to Fort Resource with his fur. You can go in with him. Or, if he'll sell you dogs and a gun, you can come back over this way. I doubt if you'd have the guts to try it, though. But any way you figure it, you'll be out of my hair for three weeks. How does it sound?"

All the bluster had drained out of Bruce McIvor's face. He licked his lips and said, "You mean you'd turn me loose back there on the height of land with nothing?"

"You'll have my big hunting shoes. You'll have two days' grub, so you can make it to Weymarn's."

Bruce McIvor came to his feet, turning over

his chair. "You can't do that!" he shouted. "That's murder!"

"Not quite," Frank demurred.

Bruce McIvor stared at him, searching with his eyes and finding the iron will of the man, and he knew he was licked. He suddenly lunged past the table for the door. Lute tripped him and he crashed to his knees, but he kept scrambling and grabbed his rifle, which he had leaned behind the door. It was wet with sweat, glistening and shiny as he turned it on Frank.

"I don't guess I'll go," Bruce said. His voice was a sneer, its tone triumphant.

Frank put his elbows on the table and smiled broadly. "You've got less sense than I supposed you had," Frank murmured. "All right, you've got a rifle in your hands. Go out and hook up your dogs."

Bruce didn't say anything for a moment. "You mean you'll let me go?"

"That's just what I don't mean," Frank murmured. "The minute you put that rifle down, we'll jump you — all three of us."

Bruce considered this for a moment as the others watched him.

Frank went on, "Even supposing you get your dogs hooked up, you won't get far. I just fed them. They'll get sick. They'll play out on you and then you can wait, with no grub, with no bedroll, for us to come after you. That ought to be fun in the dark."

Bruce regarded him with a wild and rash

anger in his dark eyes.

Frank went on placidly, "Or, if you don't think you can hook up the dogs, my shoes are outside. Take them, and try to make Lobstick with no grub, no bedroll, and us following you on the trail you'll break for us."

Lute laughed mockingly, and still Bruce didn't take his gaze from Frank's lean face.

"Or," Frank finished idly, "you can shoot us. And you haven't got the guts for that."

He turned his head away then and said, "Charlie, let's roll in. We'll start early tomorrow."

He looked over his shoulder at Bruce, who was still holding the rifle on him. "When you've made up your mind not to do it, McIvor, you better clean that gun and put it outside. A gun sweats in a warm shack. It's not good for it."

Bruce McIvor's anger broke then. Cursing wildly, he slammed the rifle to the floor. He was helpless, and he knew it, and he poured a torrent of abuse at them. He reminded Frank of a child in a tantrum, and he listened with a faint amusement. When Bruce had talked himself out, Frank said, "Take the top bunk, McIvor. We're getting up early tomorrow."

Bruce sulked a moment longer, then crossed the room and climbed into his bunk.

Frank turned to Lute. "Do you think you can stay awake tonight?"

"Sure. Why?"

"You sit up and keep watch, just in case he gets ideas. It'll be a long trick, but Charlie and

88

I need the rest and you can sleep tomorrow. That all right with you?"

"Absolutely," Lute said.

When they had all turned in, Lute shaded the lamp, took down a book from the half dozen on the wall shelf, saw it was a Modern Library *Don Quixote*, grunted with pleasure, and sat down at the table.

He moved the packsack and the pile of grub off to one side of the table, asked, "That light in your eyes?" got the answer that it wasn't, and settled down to reading.

Silence filled the night; the only sounds were the distant crack of frost splitting the trees and the patient gnawing of the dogs on their half-frozen meat outside. Presently Lute ceased turning the pages and listened carefully. He picked out Frank's deep breathing and Charlie's light exhaling. In half an hour, during which he didn't turn a page and only stared at the book, he heard Bruce McIvor's restless moaning.

Still Lute didn't move; he stared at the book, not seeing it, and gave himself to the bleak solitude of his thoughts. His eyes were dark and somber now, and his face had a set bitterness that deepened as the minutes went on.

He sighed deeply then, and looked up from his book, listening. There was sudden decision in his face now. He rose, stoked the fire, and stood by the stove, again listening. He picked out the three separate and rhythmical sounds of the sleepers' breathing; then, satisfied, he moved quietly over to the supply shelves. From one of them he took down an opened sack of flour and leaned it against the table leg.

He paused again, making sure of the same rhythm of breathing, and then he stepped over to the bookshelf where the bottle of strychnine sat. He took the bottle.

Back at the table, he settled in the chair, and holding the bottle in his hand, regarded it a long time, as if reluctant to move.

When he did move, it was to take from Bruce's supplies the small sack of sugar, which held about a cup, and untie its drawstring. Then he carefully drew the cork of the strychnine bottle. Shielding his movements by his body, he quickly dumped the strychnine into the pack of sugar, tied the drawstring, and then kneaded the sack, afterward putting it back by the other grub.

From the flour sack at his feet, it was only a moment's work to take enough flour to fill the strychnine bottle again. That done, he returned the flour sack to the supply shelf and the bottle to the bookshelf.

He stopped then, just out of the circle of lamplight, and looked at the grub on the table. He seemed satisfied.

Before he sat down again to lose himself in Don Quixote's Spain, he burned the letter that had been brought to him that afternoon.

An hour before dawn Lute rolled them out of their blankets. Bruce sulked on the edge of the bunk while Charlie and Lute rustled up breakfast. Frank loaded the sled in the raw cold that precedes daylight. They ate and afterward Charlie loaded the meager supplies into Bruce's packsack and strapped it. This would be their parting gift to Bruce on the height of land.

There was nothing left now except to lash the load and hook up the dogs, and Frank, Lute, and Charlie made short work of that. Finished, Frank went into the shack. Presently Bruce came out, his face sullen. He wordlessly accepted his snowshoes, put them on, and headed up the valley. Charlie, rifle over shoulder, followed him.

Frank gave last-minute instructions to Lute. "Lock up the shack, Lute, and take all the dogs over to Swan Lake and camp there till we get back. You can mosey over to the river trail every couple of days to see if anybody has passed on the way to the shack."

"What's that for?" Lute asked.

"It's to hide Bruce's dogs in case anybody should come up. If they see them, they'll wonder why they're here, and that'll start it. Will you do it?"

"Of course."

Frank yelled at the dogs and cracked his whip. The team snaked out into the breaking day and was soon lost in the spruce.

Lute, smiling a little, stepped back into the shack. He shivered a little and walked over to the stove, putting his back to it. His eyes raised naturally to the bookshelf.

The bottle was gone.

For perhaps a full minute he stared at the spot where the bottle should have been. And then, understanding that one of these three had taken it, he began to laugh silently, pleased with the strange ways of Providence.

Chapter Six

Bonnie was at the cigar counter writing out the dinner menus when the door opened. She didn't look up, but went on with her work. Suddenly aware that whoever came in had paused there at the counter, she glanced up from her work. Kelcy McIvor was facing her.

Bonnie said gravely, "Hello, Miss McIvor."

"Good morning," Kelcy said. Her cheeks were flushed with the cold and she smiled warmly. "It smells good in here." Her manner was shy and uneasy and determined.

Bonnie, seeing it, smiled. "Bill's making bread this morning."

There was an awkward pause then, and Kelcy laid her mittens on the counter and unbelted her mackinaw. When she looked up Bonnie was watching her with a calm secretive hostility.

"I'd — like some Gold Flakes," Kelcy said.

Bonnie shook her head and smiled faintly. "Sorry. They're a little too tony for our trade."

Kelcy said impulsively, "I don't really want cigarettes. I came to talk to you, and — well, I didn't know how to begin."

"I guess the easiest way is just to begin," Bonnie said slowly.

Kelcy smiled. "Don't think I'm snooping, but

I've heard Bruce speak about you so much."

"Not in front of your father, I dare say."

This brought a flush to Kelcy's cheeks, but she went on doggedly. "That's why I've come to see you. Do you know where Bruce is?"

Bonnie eyed her calmly. "No, I don't. You're welcome to look upstairs if you don't believe me."

"I do. Only, he hasn't been home for four days."

Bonnie shrugged. "Maybe he's gone hunting."

"He took the dogs and a gun. But somehow I don't think he's hunting."

"He didn't tell me, if that's what you were wondering. And you were, weren't you?"

Kelcy nodded.

Bonnie repeated calmly, "He didn't tell me."

Kelcy looked at her searchingly and took up her mittens. "Thank you," she said quietly. "I didn't mean to pry." She hesitated. "Do you suppose Saul knows where he's gone?"

"You might ask him."

"Is he here?"

Bonnie shook her head, and Kelcy thanked her stiffly and went out.

Bonnie went back to her work. She wrote haltingly, with concentration, for perhaps a half hour. Two customers had a late breakfast and stopped to chat with her, interrupting her work. She was returning to it when Saul tramped in. He wore a heavy horse-hide coat that was rimed at the collar with frost from his breath, and he stopped at the counter to unbutton it.

"The kid been in?" he asked.

Bonnie said no, and Saul scowled. "Where the hell is he?" He looked carefully at her. "Losin' your touch, Bonnie?"

"A man can choke on too much cake," Bonnie answered.

Saul's pouting lips thinned out. "You're funny," he said, "but not very."

He tramped on through the restaurant and went upstairs. Bonnie came to a sudden decision. She put her work away and followed him.

When she came into his room, Saul was unlacing his boots, sitting on the bed. Bonnie put her shoulder against the doorframe, placed a hand on her hip, and watched Saul in silence.

Presently she said, "The kid is up at Nearing's on Wailing River."

Saul straightened up slowly, and didn't say anything for a moment. "Since when?" he asked.

"Four days ago."

Saul came to his feet and crossed over to her, facing her. Bonnie didn't change her expression or attitude, but she watched him carefully.

"Who said?"

"I figured it out myself."

A sudden wrath crawled into Saul's eyes. He put a hand on her shoulder and swung her into the room, then slammed the door. Bonnie stood there defiantly, rubbing her shoulder.

"A fast one," Saul murmured. "Tell Papa, now."

"That's all there is to it!" Bonnie flared. "Frank

95

Nearing went in to see Kelcy McIvor with that poison he took from Joe. Kelcy climbed all over Bruce and he was mad. I came in just after they'd fought and Bruce was stealing a letter of Frank Nearing's. I saw him open it, and then he told me he was going to deliver the letter."

"The damned fool," Saul said softly, bitterly. His hot eyes were on Bonnie. "What was in it?"

"I didn't want to know."

"Why didn't you tell me that night?"

Bonnie said defiantly, "Why should I?"

"Because it's a prison offense to open mail! If he's caught, if Nearing complains, the kid will be arrested. And if he's in a jam, he'd spill everything he knows about us! I could have stopped him!"

"I'm not simple," Bonnie said calmly.

Saul stared at her, puzzled, detecting a new note in the conversation but not understanding it.

Bonnie said suddenly, "How long do you think you can kick me around, Saul?"

"Go on," Saul said, quiet menace in his voice.

"All right, I did it to scare hell out of you!" Bonnie flashed. "What do you think of that?"

Saul said, "Pretty," very softly, and did not smile.

"Maybe you can see what I've been telling you, now!" Bonnie said harshly. "That kid's been carrying your head around in a basket, and you haven't seen it! No, you've got to moon around his sister, you big slob, when we both ought to pull out of here while we can! How can you trust a kid like that, Saul? Are you going to hang around here until he gives us away, just because his sister smiles at you?" Her face was twisted with anger. "Maybe you like jail and your memories, but I don't!"

Saul's hand lashed out and slapped across Bonnie's mouth with a brutal force. It knocked her against the dresser and she fell, and some bottles on the dresser top tinkled over.

She put a hand to her mouth, and her eyes were wide with fright and surprise.

Saul said thinly, "I don't know why I don't unscrew your head, baby."

Bonnie shrank against the dresser, and Saul cursed her in a level, passionate voice. She was afraid he was going to kick her, but he didn't.

When he was finished, he said harshly, "Get up!"

Bonnie came to her feet, shaken and afraid.

Saul said, "I don't know how this will turn out, baby, but if they touch me I'll kick you all the way back to Skid Row. And you don't have enough teeth left in your face to earn your living as a hooker."

Bonnie didn't say anything; she was more afraid than angry, and more shocked than either. She knew Saul was a rough man, that underneath his workaday affability there was a hard and predatory cruelty; but that had always been reserved for somebody else. She faced it now and it was naked and raw and savage. She had overplayed

97

her hand, and Saul wouldn't spare her.

He sat down wordlessly and laced his boots again, and Bonnie watched his broad muscular back with growing concern. Finally she murmured, "I'm sorry for it, Saul. What can I do?"

Saul stood up and shrugged into his big coat. "You can go see Joe McKenzie and tell him to rig his story. Because if the kid doesn't get back here soon, the McIvors will call Millis in. Kelcy will spill the whole thing to Millis, and he'll put the screws to Joe. Tell him that."

"Where are you going?"

Saul's arrogance tipped the corner of his mouth in a faint smile. "I'm going to see the Duchess, puss. And do you know what you're going to say about it? Nothing — not one damned word."

Bonnie was afraid to argue, but the resentment and jealousy showed in her eyes. Saul stepped over and took the point of her chin between his broad fingers and pinched it and shook it cruelly. "I've been pretty good to you, puss. But keep out of my hair from now on."

He went out, and Bonnie stood there, eyes smoldering. She raised her hand tentatively to her face where he had struck her and fingered it softly.

When Saul stepped out in the cold morning, his anger was under control. The town was busy. A team hitched to the frame of a bobsled passed him, their shod hoofs ringing on the iron ice and the runners squeaking wryly under the load of logs being hauled. The horses' noses were white with frost, and they breathed long plumes of steam like storybook dragons. The dozen people on the sidewalks hurried along with short steps, heads bowed as if they were facing a wind. If a man stopped and listened, he could hear his breath crackle faintly as it froze.

Saul walked downstreet, the snow wailing under his boots, and pondered his next move. The thing he had to do now was reassure Kelcy so that her panic wouldn't drive her to Millis. There was no way of telling what the kid had done, but they'd cross that bridge when they came to it. Bonnie was right, he thought sourly; the kid was carrying their heads around in a basket. Now all he could do was stall for time until Bruce showed up. That would be easy enough, too, for Kelcy trusted him and believed in him. There was a girl, he thought fondly. She wasn't like her cheap phony of a brother; she had class and looks and a kind of bedrock honesty — the kind that money couldn't buy. He thought of her with hunger and respect and a gentle friendly contempt. She was a child, a pretty child, but she would make a man a wife that could bring envy into the eyes of a king. He dismissed that thought immediately, the longing still lingering as he mounted the steps to McIvor's store and stamped the nonexistent snow from his boots.

Inside, Mr. McIvor, a thin, kindly Scot with dead-white hair and full mustache, was waiting on trade. Saul saw Kelcy on the other side of the store, and he went over to her. She smiled when she greeted him, and Saul said, "I'm after some inside mittens — two pair."

Kelcy got them for him, and when she came back Saul said, "Well, did Bruce get his caribou?"

Kelcy looked up at him quickly. "Caribou? Is that where he is, Saul?"

"Hunting? Yes." A pause. "Didn't he tell you?"

Kelcy laughed shakily. "I went down to the restaurant today to ask Bonnie where he was. He's been gone four days. Bonnie said she didn't know where he was."

Saul smiled and shook his head. "Bonnie's a queer one. She knew, of course."

"She doesn't like me, Saul."

"Naturally." Saul laughed. "Bonnie's a nice girl, Kelcy, but she's suspicious of anybody better than a hasher. Also, she's fond of the kid and knows she shouldn't be, and that makes her uneasy with you."

"Is — is she a good person, Saul?"

Saul considered this a moment, and then said, "Well, do you think I'm a good person?"

"Of course."

"Then she is. She's straight as a string, and with her own kind they don't come better." He laughed, and there was a faint embarrassment in his laughter. "Bonnie and I are a lot alike. I understand her."

Kelcy sat on the counter now and said, "Alike?"

"We both started from the bottom of the heap. We've stepped on a few necks getting where we are. We're both rough, ignorant, and" — he smiled wryly — "a little afraid of our betters, maybe."

Kelcy laughed then. "But you're not like that, Saul."

"I am," Saul stated solemnly. "If I hadn't been, then I wouldn't be so confounded shy about asking you if I couldn't see more of you, and take you to dances."

"Why, Saul!" Kelcy was pleased and flattered and a little embarrassed, too. "What a strange thing to say!"

"Not when you understand it. I've been a bouncer in Skid Row dance halls, and I've tended bar in some pretty tough joints. I've seen a lot of muck I'd like to forget, and for a long time I thought all women were alike. That's hard to live down, even when you can read books that tell you it isn't."

Kelcy looked at him with a frank and honest regard. She said with grave good humor, "There's a dance Saturday night, Saul. Can you square-dance?"

"There isn't any other kind for me."

"Would you like to take me?"

Saul laughed. "I would break my neck for the chance."

Kelcy laughed too. "It's a date."

Saul picked up his purchase. "Don't worry about Bruce, Kelcy. I have a notion he's borrowed a shack from Ben Hudson up on Kettle Creek. If he's had any luck, he'll wait until Ben swings around that way to help him haul down the meat.

It might be a week."

"That's a relief," Kelcy said.

Outside, Saul rammed the mittens he did not want in his coat pocket and reviewed his accomplishments. They were considerable. Kelcy was reassured, and he was taking her to the dance. Bonnie would like it or lump it. He remembered young Bruce's warning to stay away from Kelcy, and he smiled. With a mail robbery hanging over his head, the kid couldn't sing very loud or very long.

Chapter Seven

A hard three-day snow had slowed them, so that on the evening of the fifth day they lacked a half day's travel from the height of land. It had been a slow, puzzling job, this trip. Frank and Charlie had traveled it in summer, going the opposite direction, and a good part of it had been observed from under a seventy-pound pack. When the creeks petered out into streams, memory faded, and there was only the tilt of the land, the shape of the country and its gaunt bony ridges to guide them over the right portage to Horn Creek.

But on that fifth night, they were certain. It was Charlie who that afternoon had walked out onto a bare tamarack meadow, toed out his shoes, and, using one for a shovel, dug down through the snow to earth. A half-dozen small pieces of charcoal bespoke a fire in the past, and Charlie remembered it as one he had built on this salt lick to serve as a smudge while he skinned out a caribou he'd shot.

Their camp that night was on the frozen hummocks of a muskeg in a tight tangle of scrub tamarack that broke the wind. Charlie fed out the last of the dog food while Frank cut some inadequate brush for their beds and stretched the tarp behind it. Bruce was dog-weary, but more cold than tired, and he rustled wood against the bleak night ahead of them. A thin dark beard stubble shadowed his face, and in those five days his cheeks had hollowed out and his eyes grown harried. Only a stubborn pride had kept him going, for he had been forced to match the pace of two seasoned bushmen who considered it a confession of weakness ever to step on the tail-board of a loaded sled and ride.

Charlie and Frank had let him alone, and he was glad for that. Whatever ideas he had of breaking away had long since vanished. He found that this tall and taciturn man and his silent Indian companion were fighting him on their own ground. They were careful always to carry or be near the two rifles. At night they hid the shells. Other than that, he was free to do anything he liked, but on the first weary day he came to realize that he was chained to them by hunger. And by something else, too. It was fear. Once they left the trails, the blazes, and in a whole day's travel did not see a single ax mark, however gray, to tell that someone had been here before them, and he was afraid. And it was this fear of that vastness and solitude that fed his hatred for his two guardians. Nights as they lay in their bedrolls, the firelight playing on the dirty tarpaulin slanting above them, Bruce would finger the bottle of strychnine in his pocket, trying for the courage to use it. He was certain they didn't know he had it. A little of it in the food and they would be finished. But he couldn't do it; his hatred was not enough. Yet there was something he could do to them, something that would even the score. On the third night he had thought of it, and on the fourth night perfected it. Tonight was the night.

It was before they had eaten and while Charlie and Frank lay stretched out, feet to the fire, waiting for the kettle to boil, that the talk began. Bruce was sitting back against the tarp, and in a half circle away from the fire the chained dogs still gnawed at their frozen food. When they looked up, their eyes were green opals with the reflection of the firelight.

Frank said, "What do you figure to Horn Creek, Charlie?"

"Oh, a half day easy."

"We might as well leave the dogs here tomorrow and go ahead on shoes, hadn't we?"

"And hunt on the way back," Charlie agreed.

Frank looked over at Bruce, who was watching them in sullen anger. Frank only smiled and rose to turn the thawing bannock propped toward the fire. He peered at the rice in the meat kettle, saw it was done, swung the kettle off with the ax handle, threw a handful of tea into the other pot, swung it off, and their supper was ready. And in that short time, Bruce knew what he was going to do.

Bruce was careful tonight not to talk. When the bannock was passed to him, he broke off a large hunk. Charlie flipped the lard bucket to

him, Bruce smeared the bannock thickly with
lard, sprinkled it with sugar, and laid it aside.
While the other two were busy eating, he carefully
broke his piece of bannock and crammed half
of it, grease and all, into his pants pocket.

He had a vast impatience with the rest of the
evening, and it was he who first suggested hitting
the bedrolls. The hardest part would be to keep
awake, for he was dead weary. But he lay there,
face turned toward the tarp, until he heard the
others sleeping.

Then he drew out his bottle of strychnine.
Hands under the bedroll, he fumbled his crushed
piece of bannock into one hand and the uncorked
strychnine bottle into the other. He dumped the
powder onto the bannock in his hand, and then
kneaded the whole mess into a damp ball of soggy
bread. That done, he corked the bottle and put
it back in one pocket, and placed the wadded
ball of bannock in another. He went to sleep
remembering that the first thing he must do in
the morning was wash his hands thoroughly, lest
he poison himself.

Charlie had a fire going long before daylight.
They ate a hurried breakfast, cleaned up camp,
and at the first crack of dawn were ready to
start.

The dogs stood up, waiting to be hooked up.
Charlie laughed at them and they started to bark.
Bruce put on his snowshoes, feeling his heart ham-
mering.

From the cariole Frank took the packsack,

which was still strapped tightly the way Charlie had left it at the shack, and handed it to Bruce.

"Put it on. You might as well get used to it."

Bruce did, and afterward they left camp. Charlie took the lead, gun over shoulder. Bruce walked in the middle.

Fifty yards from camp, Bruce suddenly stopped. "I haven't got any tobacco."

Frank said, "Let's see."

Bruce pulled out his pouch. It was almost empty. He said, "I saw a third of a can back in the grub box. Do you care if I take that?"

"Ask Charlie. It's his," Frank said.

Charlie murmured, "Sure, take it."

Bruce turned and started back to camp. Frank and Charlie waited. When Bruce got back to camp, the dogs were all standing, eyeing him hopefully, their tails wagging. Bruce brought out his wadded ball of bannock, broke it into five pieces, and gave each dog a piece. They wolfed it down in a gulp. He would have liked to stay long enough to see the poison work, but he didn't want to make them suspicious enough to come back.

He rejoined them, said thanks to Charlie, and they started off again.

All that day, Bruce thought about the poisoned dogs. He could imagine Frank and Charlie pulling into camp tonight, tired and hungry, to find all five of their dogs dead and frozen. They would be wild. They'd have to leave their whole outfit there, stuff their pockets with not enough grub, and spend a weary week of hungry days and cold nights, maybe more, before they got back. And that was worse than he had to put up with, which was consolation.

In midmorning the land began to tilt down to the north, and in early afternoon they picked up a tiny stream fringed with stunted alders.

Charlie hauled up, and Bruce and Frank came up to him.

"There's Horn Creek," Frank said. "Follow it down. Weymarn's place is at the mouth. It ought to take you two pretty stiff days' travel."

Bruce hunched the pack up on his shoulders, and when he turned to regard them, he was almost smiling.

"How long'll it take you to make your shack?"

"Six long days," Frank said. "But I don't figure to hit the shack. We'll cut over to Lobstick, and that'll take over a week. I'm going to be there in plenty of time to get my claim letter out to the recording office."

"What are you going to do when they miss me?"

"I'll give myself time and then tell them. But I don't think anybody will miss you enough to be curious."

Bruce's haggard face flushed a little at the jibe, but his smile soon returned. "And you think it'll take you a little over a week?"

"That's right."

"Wouldn't want to bet on that, would you?"

Frank frowned. "Sure, I'll bet."

108

"Better not," Bruce drawled, grinning. He raised his mittened hand to his fur cap in mock salute. "So long. I've got a lot to even up with you, Nearing."

"You'll have plenty of time to figure out how," Frank murmured.

"And I will. Thanks for nothing." Bruce looked at Charlie and sneered. "You too," he said. They watched him until he disappeared in a stand of timber.

Then Frank said, "What was he talking about?"

Charlie shrugged and looked up at the sun. "Give me your gun and I'll bet you we have deer steak for supper." He had already forgotten Bruce.

Three miles down Horn Creek, Bruce discovered he was hungry. He built a fire, opened his pack, filled his kettle with snow, and propped his bannock up to thaw out. He could still get a laugh at the scene Frank and Charlie would find when they reached camp.

He pulled out his stolen bottle of strychnine and looked at it. It was half full. There'd been enough stuff in that wad of bannock to kill an army, he thought, putting the bottle back in his pocket.

Just before the water boiled, he broke out his lard and sugar and waited impatiently for the food that was a minute away.

Chapter Eight

Lute had a letter to mail, and the process involved some difficulty. There were ten dogs in camp, five of them Bruce's. He couldn't show up in Lobstick with Bruce's dogs, or there would be questions asked. He'd have to leave them for four days, and they'd have to be fed.

Lute was a methodical man, so he did what was necessary. He took one day's feed, multiplied it by four, then methodically placed that much meat before each of the chained dogs he was to leave.

His letter was written and in his pocket, and he set out for Lobstick, driving Charlie's dogs. That letter was to Carl, warning him never, under any circumstances, to write him again. If they were hot on his trail Carl was to radio him a code message, nothing else.

He arrived in Lobstick on a Saturday morning, chained his dogs out behind the hotel, and walked to the post office.

Stepping inside McIvor's store, he went over to the mail window, where Kelcy was.

She recognized him immediately, and barely nodded in return to his greeting.

"I would like a stamp," Lute said.

Kelcy sold him one. Lute licked it and placed

it squarely on the envelope, his manner precise and unhurried.

There was something so quietly arrogant, so unruffled, so unbending about this big man that it was like a challenge. "Were you sent down to check up on my end of the blackmail?" Kelcy asked him.

Lute finished his business with great deliberation, then handed the letter to Kelcy. "That was unfortunate," he said calmly. "I was mistaken that day about the eavesdropping."

"So you've come down to apologize."

"Not quite," Lute said stiffly. "I meant what I said, only I put it bluntly, I'm afraid."

"I'm afraid so, too," Kelcy retorted. They looked at each other a bare moment, but there was something in the man's eyes that made Kelcy look away. They should have been nice eyes, she thought later; they were a nice color of blue, clear, wide spaced, and recessed, but there was a quality of agate about them, a surface light that was as chill as glare ice. She was glad when he touched his cap and went out. Only then did she remember that she hadn't asked after Frank Nearing. Immediately after this she wondered why she had ever thought she should ask about him. It was puzzling, this feeling, and she supposed it resulted from her concern over Bruce.

Lute went down the street, seeking food. He passed up the hotel as somehow being too conspicuous, and turned into the Star Café. Taking a seat at the counter, his stomach gnawing and almost tasting the good smells, he ordered a meal and then waited patiently.

Bonnie, from behind her counter, saw him come in. She knew every man in this town, every trapper in the surrounding bush, but she did not know him. And then suddenly she remembered Saul describing this man. He was Frank Nearing's partner, the man Nearing had met at the plane that day Bruce dropped the strychnine.

Bonnie studied his profile, a faint interest stirring within her. If this was Frank Nearing's partner, and he had come down from the Wailing, where was Bruce? Bonnie considered this question a moment, more out of curiosity than concern for Bruce. What would he do if she went over and asked him? Surely he knew about the strychnine, and about Bruce's delivering the two opened letters. She thought of Saul, and how angry he would be if she did this, and then a slow anger stirred within her. She didn't care what Saul thought. This morning Saul had told her he was taking Kelcy to the dance that night. There had been an argument, and Saul had hit her again. Hard.

She came out from behind the cigar stand, a shapely, sullen-looking girl in a white wool sweater that fitted tightly across her bosom. She took a stool beside Lute, who turned his head to look at her, then looked away.

"How's Bruce?" Bonnie asked.

Lute was drinking. He finished drinking, and deliberately put down the glass. "Bruce who?"

"You're Lute Westock, aren't you? Frank Nearing's partner?"

"That's right."

"I'm talking about Bruce McIvor. He's up at your place on Wailing River, isn't he?"

Lute was a long time answering, during which interval he regarded Bonnie with an unblinking stare that was baleful and not pleasant.

"Who said he was?" Lute asked finally.

A handsome half-breed waitress in a white uniform came in with Lute's breakfast then. In front of her boss and a handsome customer, the girl was solicitous until Bonnie said impatiently, "He's all right, Mary. Beat it." The girl sulked back into the kitchen. Lute began to eat as if Bonnie weren't there.

Bonnie slid off the stool and said with faint amusement, "O.K., Stonepuss. You two guys will change your tune with Bruce now, though, won't you?"

Lute didn't even look at her, but asked, "Why?"

"You know why," Bonnie retorted. She walked back to the cigar counter, and Lute turned his head, fork poised, to look at her back. When she glanced down the counter at him again, he was eating.

Lute had two breakfasts. Finished, he came up to the register to pay his check. "You run a hotel here too?"

"That's what the sign says," Bonnie replied tartly.

"I would like to see your rooms."

Bonnie looked him up and down and said, "You're going slumming, but it's up to you."

She rang up the check, then headed for the stairs, Lute following her. She went up, passed the corridor's three closed doors, and opened the door to the end bunk room. It was clean and empty. Lute stepped past her and gave the place a brief inspection.

"I'd like something else," he said. "More private."

"That's what the other hotel was built for," Bonnie said carelessly.

"You haven't other rooms?"

"No."

Lute didn't say anything, only turned around and started down the hall. He stopped in front of a door and pointed. "This is a room, isn't it?"

"It's mine."

Lute pointed across the hall. "And this is a room also?"

Bonnie said patiently, "One room is mine, one is the boss's, and the other room is rented. We only got the big room, I told you."

Lute thought a moment and said, "I'd like to reserve a bunk in that room for tonight, then."

Bonnie laughed sardonically. "You want to reserve the whole suite, or just parlor, bedroom, and bath?"

Lute didn't smile. He said, "Bath?"

"Skip it," Bonnie said. "I'll tell the maid to

114

put on the lavender sheets."

She went down ahead of him and watched him go out. He was a humorless man, she thought, not a very pleasant one, and it wasn't because of her mood. She wouldn't even like him on Christmas.

So it was with no feeling at all that she watched him come in an hour later and say, "I've changed my mind. You can cancel my reservation. I am starting back to camp."

"Say hello to the kid for me," Bonnie murmured. "Tell him to sell out high."

Lute scowled. "I don't understand."

"I wonder," Bonnie murmured.

When Saul came in that noon, he didn't speak to Bonnie, and he went out fifteen minutes later without even nodding. By nightfall, Bonnie was in a vile temper. She rowed with the cook, and when Mary, the half-breed waitress, asked for the night off to go to the dance, Bonnie turned on her savagely. She knew what the trouble was, but she couldn't help herself. This being brave when another woman was stealing your man was all right in theory, but it didn't work out. It hurt.

Saul came in after dark and went out all dressed up and barbered, ready for the dance. Bonnie didn't even see him go, but she knew he was gone. The rush hour passed and eight o'clock came, and the waitresses were idle and sullen. And Bonnie was stubborn. At nine o'clock she couldn't stand it any longer. She took her coat off the hook and went out. She was going to look in on the dance, anyway, and see her.

Once Bonnie was gone, Mary, the waitress, went back into the kitchen to sulk. But the Chinese cook was reading a Chinese paper, and wouldn't even talk to her. The place was deserted, empty.

She wandered out into the restaurant again and tried to read, hating Bonnie all the time. She could have gone to the dance if Bonnie had let her. She thought of the dance and the dresses and of her own dress and then of Bonnie's good-looking clothes. It gave her an idea.

She made sure the cook was reading, then tip-toed up the hotel stairs, down the hall, and into Bonnie's room off the corridor. She shut the door behind her, lighted the lamp, and went over to the closet to look inside. The array of dresses pleased her, and she was standing there feasting her eyes when it happened.

She didn't hear the shot, didn't hear the glass break. Something crashed into the back of her head, and that was all.

The cook, hearing her fall, found her lying on the floor, half in and half out of the closet, blood pooling around her cheek.

He sent for Millis and for Saul.

When Millis arrived, he posted a man at the door to keep everyone out. Bonnie and Saul came later, separately, but only seconds apart. They found Millis and the doctor squatting over the half-breed girl.

Saul took a look at her, and his stomach sawed, and he said, "God! What happened?"

Bonnie was behind him. She looked at the girl and was only curious, not minding the blood.

Millis rose. He had put on his coat hurriedly, and it was buttoned crooked. His broad face was grim, and he was still wearing the shell-rimmed glasses that gave him a deceptive air of benevolence.

"Well, she never knew what hit her," he announced. He pointed to the window. "Figure it out for yourself."

Saul walked over to the window and looked at the star-shaped hole in the glass. Outside, down the alley, he could see men with lanterns moving. Bonnie stood inside the room, still staring at the girl, still not believing it.

Millis had returned to the girl. He said, "Well, Doc, I'm through. Where do you want her?"

Afterward he went to the foot of the stairs and called for two men, and then came back upstairs. He said to Saul, "Where can we talk?"

Saul and Bonnie took him into the bunk room. They sat at the table, while Millis unbuttoned his coat and shoved his glasses in the pocket. A knock came on the door and a man said, "It was the barbershop shed roof. He scraped the snow clean, so there weren't any tracks."

"No sign?"

"Nothing. Not even the cartridge case."

Millis thanked him and closed the door. He came over, hands rammed in hip pockets, and

117

said suddenly to Saul, "Between me and you, she was on the turf, wasn't she?"

"I don't know," Saul answered.

"I do. She's had the breeds following her like a dog follows —" His voice trailed off, out of respect to Bonnie.

Bonnie said, "But I don't understand. Why was she killed in my room?"

Millis hauled up abruptly and stared at Bonnie. "Oh? You say it's your room?"

"Yes. What did she want in there?"

Millis still looked at her, his eyes musing, and he was silent for a long time. Then he murmured, "So that's it." He walked slowly over to Bonnie. "Has this girl ever stolen?"

"Not that I know of."

Millis grunted and turned away. He circled the room twice, head bowed in thought, hands rammed in hip pockets. On the third time around he stopped in front of Bonnie and asked idly, "Know anybody that would like to see you dead, Miss Tucker?"

Bonnie opened her mouth in surprise, closed it, then said faintly, "See me dead?"

"It's your room," Millis said brusquely. "Your hair is black. From the roof of the barbershop woodshed, all dark women would look alike. Whoever put that shot in there didn't have Mary in mind." He paused. "He had you in mind."

The doctor opened the door then and said, "Come here a minute, Millis."

Millis went out, leaving Bonnie and Saul alone.

Across the table, under the overhead lamp, they looked at each other. Saul finally said, "That's hooey, what Millis said. Who'd shoot at you?"

Bonnie licked her lips and said faintly, "Sure. It's hooey."

But it wasn't. Millis' question, "Know anybody who'd like to see you dead?" was still in her ears. And the answer to it was in her mind. "Bonnie, if you're lying to me, I'll kill you, so help me!" Bruce had said that, and he meant it, and she had lied to him. But he was at Wailing River — or was he? Lute Westock this morning had denied it. Couldn't Bruce be right here, now?

Saul said curiously, "Why, Bonnie, you're shivering."

Bonnie was, and not from the chill of the room.

Chapter Nine

It took Frank and Charlie six and a half days to make it back from the height of land to Lobstick. With no traps to tend, they had swung east to the lakes, and had come down the old fur portage to the Raft. Behind them two days of snow had blotted out their trail. Ahead of them, in Lobstick, Frank didn't know what they'd find.

The whole town might be in an uproar over Bruce McIvor's disappearance. They even might have investigated Christmas Valley. If Lute had followed instructions to camp with Bruce McIvor's team out on Swan Lake away from the shack and anyone who might question Bruce's disappearance, they were still reasonably safe. Of course, Christmas Valley was open to any snooper now, but that risk was preferable to having Bruce McIvor free to talk. Frank had made his choice, and time would tell if he had made the right one.

They swung into Lobstick at noon on the tail end of the long snow, and the stores already had men clearing the walks. Frank waved tentatively at a couple of them, and they waved back indifferently. Apparently nobody was looking for him and Charlie. Once he saw a woman on the sidewalk stop and stare at them as they passed, but that might have been only idle curiosity.

They put up their dogs behind the hotel, got a room, and ate their midday meal in the dining room, and still nobody challenged them.

Afterward Frank borrowed pen and paper from the desk and went up to his room to write his letter. The mail had gone out yesterday, so he had a whole week in which to write the letter recording his claim. But somehow it seemed imperative to him to get it done. The day for which he had been waiting all these months was approaching. This was an act of faith.

He rolled a cigarette and leaned back in his chair, match held idly in his hand. For a moment he contemplated the blank sheet of paper, knowing what he was going to write, even down to the phrasing of the letter. He'd spent a hundred nights memorizing it, polishing it, perfecting it. The result was a dry statement of fact, naming corners and locations, along with a note pointing out the forfeiture of the previous claim.

He lighted his cigarette, picked up the pen in his blunt, scarred hands, and dipped it in the ink.

There was a knock on the door.

Frank cursed soundlessly, came to his feet, and walked across the room, his moccasins making no noise at all.

He opened the door and Corporal Millis, coat under arm, confronted him. Frank managed a civil greeting, and Millis said indifferently, "Busy, Nearing?"

"Nothing that can't wait. Come in."

Millis walked into the room and threw his coat and fur cap on the bed. There was a certain harried expression lurking in his mild eyes as he took the old rocker and looked about the room. Frank sat at the desk, watching him drum his fingers on the chair arm, and thought, This is it. He knows Bruce came to us. Be careful.

Millis said, "Haven't seen you around."

"I'm not much for town," Frank said.

"Heard what's been happening here, then?"

"No. I just got in."

"There's been a murder here since I saw you last."

Frank relaxed, and found he'd been holding his breath. It wasn't trouble, then; Millis just wanted to unburden himself. Frank asked who had been murdered, and Millis told him a breed girl over at the Star Café had been shot, and he related the circumstances.

"Queer thing is," Millis went on, "she was killed by mistake, I think. The shot was intended for Bonnie Tucker, the girl that runs the restaurant. Know her?"

Frank said he didn't, and asked, "Arrested anybody?"

Millis stretched his legs out in front of him and said mildly, "Didn't even have a lead until today." He looked briefly at Frank and then at his boots. "I thought maybe you could help me out."

"I'd be glad to, but how can I?"

Millis tilted his head back and looked at the ceiling and rubbed his chin, and the faint beginnings of suspicion again stirred within Frank. Millis was circling the subject, but he had his eye on it.

"This Bonnie Tucker saw you and this Indian come into town today. She came right to me."

That was the woman who stared at them on the street, Frank guessed. He said, "What have I got to do with it?"

"Wait," Millis said. "Let's go back to what she told me. She said she'd been thinking about that girl's death, and how the killer meant that bullet for her. She said there was a man who might kill her if he got mad enough, but she'd thought that man was away from Lobstick when the crime was committed. Now she isn't so sure."

"Who is the man?" Frank asked slowly.

Millis looked at him then. "Bruce McIvor."

Frank reached over to the desk and carefully doused his cigarette, and when he turned to Millis again, his face was impassive. "And he wasn't away at the time?"

"Was he?" Millis asked gently.

Here it was. Millis knew, and so long as he knew there was no use denying it. The thing to do was quiet Millis' suspicion immediately, before it gathered momentum.

Frank looked at him blankly for several seconds, and then smiled and said, "Oh, I get it. You mean you want to know when I last saw McIvor. It was a week ago. When did the murder happen?"

"Tell me first how long you were with him."

"Six days, a week."

"All the time?"

"Every second. When did the murder happen?"

"During that week," Millis said. "Where is he now?"

"He left my place heading for the height of land," Frank said. It was the truth, but not all of it.

Millis' eyes opened. "The height of land? What's he doing out there?"

"I guess you'd have to ask him," Frank said idly.

There was a lot more Millis wanted to ask. He wasn't satisfied and Frank knew it, and he could almost see Millis thinking there were some things here that didn't shape up right. But Frank had answered his questions, and Millis couldn't ask more without exceeding his authority for the present. Millis rose and picked up his coat and fur cap.

"I'll go talk to the girl," Millis said. "You'll be around, won't you?"

"As long as you want me," Frank said easily.

When Millis had gone, Frank sat on the bed, his mind working swiftly. The whole setup was risky. It reminded him of a sweater, with Millis holding a single thread. If Millis chose to yank that thread, the whole sweater would unravel. He came to his feet and started to pace the floor. Should he get hold of Charlie and warn him? No, Millis would be watching for that, and it would deepen his suspicion. Besides, when Charlie was confronted with strangers he was an Indian again, and he acted like a harmless idiot, silent, sullen, dumb. And Lute? If he had followed orders, he was on Swan Lake, with a dozen snows to cover his trail.

Frank fought down his excitement and tried to think what Millis would do. Millis had to be satisfied with Frank's alibi for Bruce McIvor, since Charlie would back him up. But would his curiosity and suspicion prod him on to asking questions about Bruce's whereabouts that Frank couldn't or wouldn't answer?

And immediately, Frank was reminded of the job that Millis had interrupted. That letter was the most important. Once that was off, he could lie, deceive, and stall for the precious week he needed. Afterward, the truth could out and nobody would be harmed.

He sat down at the desk and carefully wrote out his claim. He had finished when there was a timid knock on the door. It was the clerk, who said, "Corporal Millis asked if you'd step over to the Star Café."

Frank thanked him and said he was on his way. He shrugged into his parka and went downstairs, got an envelope and stamp, and addressed and mailed his letter.

Afterward he cut across the street to the Star. The waitress directed him upstairs to the bunk room. When he knocked Millis' voice bade him enter.

He stepped inside. The overhead lamp was lighted against the dusk, and around the table beneath it sat Kelcy McIvor and a girl Frank did not know. Millis had just turned from the window. Charlie, holding a thin cigarette between his fingers, was seated on the bunk. Frank did not look at him. He spoke to Kelcy, and then Millis introduced him to Bonnie Tucker, who barely nodded to him. She was a handsome vivid girl with a sudden defiance in her eyes, but beside Kelcy's blonde, calm serenity, she seemed lush and hard. Frank pulled off his parka while Millis sank into one chair and kicked another toward Frank.

"It's too cold to keep running from one of you to the next," Millis said bluntly. "Besides, I want you all together, where I can remember what you're saying. Miss Tucker, you came to see me this afternoon. Tell them why."

Kelcy's golden hair caught light from the lamp and glowed with a live sheen as she watched Bonnie.

"If you want her to hear, I should worry," Bonnie said to Millis, nodding to Kelcy. She turned to look at Kelcy then. "I told Millis I think Bruce killed that girl, thinking it was me."

"Bruce?" Kelcy echoed faintly. Then her voice firmed with instant anger. "That's not so! Why would he want to kill you?"

Bonnie's lip lifted faintly. "You're asking for it, so here goes. Bruce was jealous of Saul. He told me once if he thought Saul would take me

126

from him, he'd kill me. Well, Saul can have me any time, and the kid knows it. How do you like that?"

"I don't mind it at all," Kelcy said angrily, her face flushed, "except that it doesn't explain anything."

"No?" Bonnie looked at Frank and then back at Kelcy. "Where was Bruce the night Mary was killed?"

"Hunting, wasn't he?"

"He was not. He was going to Nearing's on Wailing River, so he said. But Nearing and that Siwash came in today without him. Then where is Bruce?"

Both Kelcy and Bonnie looked at Frank. "He was there a week with me," Frank explained. "He was with me when that girl was killed."

"Who says so?" Bonnie asked sharply. "You do, and maybe that Siwash does. I don't believe it."

"Why would they lie for him?" Millis asked slowly.

Bonnie looked searchingly at Frank. "He knows. Ask him what Bruce talked about when he got up there."

For a moment Frank stared at her, and then his face got stiff with anger. The recorder's letter! She knew, too. He said softly, angrily, swiftly, "Bruce is still loose, Miss Tucker. Maybe you better be careful of what he wouldn't want known."

"What's that?" Millis said sharply.

Frank kept looking at Bonnie. "Ask her. She seems to know."

"Nothing," Bonnie said sullenly, after a long pause.

Millis looked from Bonnie to Frank, and back to Bonnie, a hard exasperation in his face. "Somebody better make sense about this," he said grimly. "I don't care which one of you does it."

"I don't either," Bonnie said defiantly. "All I want to tell you is that Bruce was the one who shot that girl! I tell you, it couldn't have been anybody else!"

"Wrong," Frank murmured.

"You're a liar!" Bonnie said hotly.

Frank shrugged and glanced at Kelcy. She was watching him with an unblinking, breathless concentration.

Then Kelcy said, "This argument doesn't make sense. If Bruce was with Nearing when Mary Paulin was killed, he couldn't have killed her."

"But was he?" Bonnie said sharply. "Where is he?"

Kelcy looked at Frank. "Where is he?"

"Across the height of land," Frank said.

A subtle, indefinable suspicion crept into Kelcy's eyes. "The height of land? Why is he back there?"

"You'd better ask him," Frank said shortly. "He stayed with us a week, then headed for the height of land."

"When?" Bonnie asked.

"A week ago."

"After the murder!" Bonnie said triumphantly, looking at Millis. "Doesn't that prove to you he's running away?"

Frank said flatly, with what he hoped was finality, "He wasn't outside my sight for a week, I tell you." He turned and said to Charlie, "Tell them, Charlie."

"He was with us," Charlie said softly.

Frank glanced at the others. Bonnie was regarding Millis with a challenging glance, and Millis looked angrily bewildered. Only Kelcy was looking at Frank; she had never taken her glance from him.

She said calmly, "Bruce hated the bush, and he hated you! He wouldn't go to your place or back to the height of land. Where is he?"

"See?" Bonnie jeered.

Kelcy turned on Bonnie and spoke passionately. "You little fool, keep still! Bruce didn't shoot at you, and you know it! We all do! I'm trying to find out where he is!"

Millis said flatly, "Keep quiet, both of you."

There was a long silence, during which Kelcy never took her eyes from Frank. Then she said flatly, "Something has happened to Bruce."

Frank's eyes glinted unpleasantly. "Be careful," he said softly.

"I tell you, something has happened to Bruce," Kelcy repeated defiantly. She looked at Millis now.

A hot anger stirred in Frank. This girl's persistence was slowly and surely dragging him into

129

real danger. He could tell Millis that Bruce was peddling strychnine, and watch Kelcy squirm. And then he was ashamed of the thought — and still angry.

Kelcy stood up now, real alarm in her face. "Bruce hasn't been home for more than two weeks! Bonnie says he started for Nearing's and Nearing admits he saw him! And now Bruce is gone — back to the height of land! I don't believe it. Corporal Millis, I've got a right to ask you to find Bruce!"

"All right, all right," Millis said patiently.

"But it's not all right!" Kelcy cried. "What if they've murdered him? What if his body is lying in the snow right now up by Nearing's shack? How do you know it isn't?"

"Why would Nearing kill him?" Millis asked savagely. "Why in hell would he want to?"

Kelcy's glance shuttled to Frank. Here it comes, Frank thought. She'll spill it all. She'll tell him about Lute's blackmail of her, and my blackmail of Bruce. And Millis will bust it wide open, the mine and all of it.

A kind of fear came into Kelcy's eyes then, and vanished, and Frank waited breathlessly for her to go on.

"I don't know," she said grimly. "But I know something's wrong, something is terribly wrong! Bruce hated the bush! If a person is lost, you have to look for him, don't you? Don't you?"

Millis sighed. Frank felt relief flood over him and make him weak. She was afraid to tell the whole story. But her stubborn insistence that Millis look for Bruce was almost as bad. He'd have to stop that; he'd have to take her to Bruce before her fear for his safety overcame her fear for his good name. Above all, he must keep them away from Christmas Valley.

There was derision in his voice as he said, "I'd be glad to guide you. He's probably at Weymarn's crossing at this moment. That's ten days or two weeks away by dog team, but go have a look."

"Make him prove it," Kelcy said swiftly to Millis.

Millis glared at Frank. "Is he there?"

"He's there," Frank said bitterly, "but have I got to bring back his ear to prove it?"

Kelcy ignored that, and talked to Millis. "Just what do I have to do to make you find Bruce?"

Millis sighed. "Any reasonable proof that he's lost will start a search party. But is he lost?"

Kelcy said swiftly, "I don't know, but I know something has happened to him. He's not strong enough to cross the height of land. He can't hunt like a bush trapper! He couldn't make it there. If he isn't there, will Frank be arrested?"

"One thing at a time," Millis said wearily. "Let me think."

But Kelcy couldn't be stopped. All the days of bitter wonder where Bruce was, all of Saul's easy assurances that secretly she had come to disbelieve, all the fear had burst the dam of her reticence. She said swiftly, "Look, Corporal Millis. If Dad pays the cost of a plane, can we fly over to Weymarn's? If it takes two weeks to get there by dog team, he may be dead!"

Millis was baffled. Her fear was close to stampeding him, but when he reasoned it away, there was still some doubt left. He looked at her, at the silent pleading in her face, and came to a decision.

"Of course we can fly. I'll radio out tonight for a plane, if your father insists."

Kelcy straightened up and looked at Frank. "And you'll come with us."

She went out the door. Frank rose and followed her out. At the head of the stairwell he caught up with her. She turned to face him there.

"Beautiful," he said wryly, his voice shaky with anger, "go ahead with it. Only remember one thing, Miss McIvor, and I'll give it to you with the bark on. I took Bruce over to the height of land. I admit it. He's safe there. But if he doesn't keep his mouth shut when we reach him, I'll turn him in!"

There was a long silence, then Kelcy said in a harsh, unbending voice, "If I find Bruce, it's all I care about."

Millis opened the door then, and the shaft of light from the room struck Kelcy's face. It was grim and strained and afraid, and she went down the stairs. Frank walked back for his parka. Millis met him in the hall, and Millis hauled up beside him.

"Remember what I told you that night in my office, Nearing?" he asked. His broad honest face was stern, his eyes heavy with censure.

"I remember."

"Well, you're paying for turning down some good advice. The hell of it is I'm paying for you, too. What did you take McIvor over there for?"

"I never said I did."

Millis glared at him, baffled and angry. "What did he come up to see you for?"

"He — just came."

"You're dodging something," Millis said grimly. "I'll find out what it is, too, before I'm finished. Now I want a straight answer to this question. Could Bruce have killed Mary Paulin?"

"Not possibly."

Millis grunted and went on down the stairs.

Frank stepped into the room. Bonnie was still seated at the table, and she was watching him. Frank put on his parka and came over to the table, looking across it down at her.

"I meant what I said about Bruce," he murmured. "He didn't do it."

Bonnie said bitterly, "I wish I'd read that letter Bruce stole when I had the chance. I'd know soon enough if you were lying for him because he had something on you."

Frank wanted to laugh with relief. She didn't know what was in the recorder's letter, after all; she'd been bluffing, and bluffing well.

But her suspicion had led to this questioning, and this questioning to Kelcy's panic, which would lead to their finding Bruce. And then he was just where he had started back in the shack.

Bruce wouldn't talk about the mine; he'd be afraid to with the mail-robbery charge hanging over him. Kelcy would stop him. But he would be back where liquor and friends might pry it out of him, and the old risk was there.

Frank said wryly, "Someday you'll come to me and say you're sorry for this. I'll laugh at it then, but it isn't very funny now, sister. It isn't funny at all."

Chapter Ten

After his shave and haircut that night, Frank stepped into the rear room of the barbershop, which Old Man Cooper had turned into a bathroom. It was a small room, oven-warm, barely large enough to hold the big zinc tub, the rickety old range whose draft was chuttering away now, and the lone chair. The new khaki coveralls, the sheep-lined overshoes, the whole new outfit from the skin out that he had bought earlier in the evening was still wrapped and on the chair, and the tub was filled with steaming water. Two dollars had bought Old Man Cooper and his shop for a whole evening, and Frank meant to enjoy them.

He took an hour with his bath, letting the heat loosen his trail-tautened muscles and flow through him like some rich drug. His eyes were closed, his body submerged up to the chin, and he was on the thin edge of sleep when he heard the door open.

Charlie stepped in and shut the door, and Frank heaved himself to a sitting position.

"Where's Cooper?" Charlie said.

"Sitting in the barber chair reading, isn't he?"

Charlie shook his head and lowered his voice. "I just saw one of Bruce McIvor's dogs."

135

Frank stared at him a moment and then said, "Loose?"

Charlie nodded. "He must have broke away from Lute up on Swan Lake."

Frank reached for a towel and climbed out of the tub, drying himself rapidly. They both knew why Charlie thought the presence of this dog was important. If somebody recognized the dog and the word got around to Kelcy, they would be hard put to explain why the dog, supposedly at Weymarn's crossing with Bruce, was here. In her almost hysterical frame of mind, Kelcy would go to Millis and insist that Frank was lying about Bruce's whereabouts and demand an investigation. And the obvious result of that would be a trip to Christmas Creek, not to Weymarn's crossing.

Frank swore softly as he climbed into his clothes. At all costs they must catch that dog and hide him until the plane left tomorrow noon. This picture of himself scheming wildly to undo what he had spent two weeks accomplishing brought a wry smile to Frank's face. It was plan, retreat, cover-up, lie, stall, and compromise until the claim deadline was reached. Two days spent in picking up Bruce would cut the time until the plane left with the claim letter to five days, and if necessary he would stay with him every minute until the week was out. But if this dog were found and Millis headed for Christmas Valley with a search party in a plane to discover the mine, it would leave days in which anybody could file a counter-claim. The best bet was to head for Weymarn's crossing, so the dog must be caught and hidden.

Charlie was waiting for him out in the shop. Frank left two dollars for Cooper and stepped out into the night. An occasional store lamp faintly lighted the street. The snow still held on.

The dog wasn't where Charlie had last seen him, so he and Frank started their patrol in the dark. They walked up to the head of the street, crossed over, and came down the other side. And then, just across from the Star Café they saw the dog. He was standing in the middle of the road, head lifted, watching the door to the Star Café, a medium-sized gray-blue dog with a magnificent plumed tail.

They stopped and Frank called the dog, who looked toward them, not wagging his tail. Frank began to walk toward him slowly, talking softly to him. When he got into the light from the windows of the café, the dog's tail dropped and he began to sidle away, his eyes suspicious.

Suddenly a voice close to him said, "It won't work, Frank."

It was Lute's voice. Frank moved out of the light and over to the edge of the building, and there was Lute in the shadows.

"What are you doing down here?"

"Chasing that damn dog!" Lute said viciously. "I've trailed him all the way down from Swan Lake. I had a choke collar on him and he pawed it over his ears and hit for town."

"Anybody been up to the shack?" Frank asked quickly.

"There was a clean trail from this side," Lute said.

Charlie came up then. He and Lute didn't speak to each other. The three of them stood there in the deep shadow of the restaurant watching the dog out in the slowly falling snow, and they were helpless.

Frank swore and said, "We've got to get him. It's my neck if we don't."

They stepped into the light now to follow the dog, who was walking slowly down the road. Frank looked obliquely at Lute. Outside of the pale beard stubble on his face, he had that neat, scrubbed, capable look, as always. It suddenly occurred to Frank that Lute had been as helpful as a man could be, outside of that first blunder that antagonized Kelcy. Certainly he was doing all he could to help Frank keep his secret, and it didn't matter much whether it was through fear or the desire to be helpful. Frank asked, "When did he break loose?"

"Yesterday morning."

"And you've been trailing him all day and night?"

"That's right." Lute looked at him. "You told me to watch them closely, but I couldn't help it, Frank. I even took a shot at him, but he was too far away when I tried."

"Forget it," Frank said brusquely. "Let's get him. If he's been going a day and a night, he's hungry. Charlie, you go get some of our moose meat out of the shed. Lute and I will keep an eye on him."

Charlie cut across the street, heading for the shed behind the hotel. He skirted the dog, who looked incuriously at him, and then away.

Afterward the dog lifted his head to keen the air. Somebody was coming down the walk. Frank and Lute put their shoulders against the side of the building, as if talking, and the man passed them, spoke, and vanished in the night down the street.

There was a grim humor in all this that Frank didn't miss. One damned dog, scared and hungry and bewildered, could touch off a powder train that would explode at Christmas Creek and wreck everything.

The dog moved now. He keened the air again and gauged their nearness to him. Then he started off down the narrow snow-packed walk that ran along the side of the Star Café to its rear. Frank and Lute dropped in behind him.

They were halfway down the walk when hell's own din broke loose somewhere back of the café. A dozen dogs started to bark and snarl in wild rage, and Frank knew the cause. A chained sled dog at sight of a free dog will go almost crazy with anger, and Bruce's dog had been spied by some chained dogs in the rear.

He moved swiftly to the back of the restaurant, Lute behind him. The din increased in fury. Bruce's dog, faintly outlined against the snow, stood beside a heavy wire pen inside which a dozen dogs were chained and raving.

Now was the time to surprise the dog. Frank started out slowly, soundlessly, across the thirty yards of hard-packed snow. He and Lute were halfway across the strip when the rear door of the restaurant suddenly opened and a lantern lighted up the night.

Frank wheeled. There, standing on the steps holding the lantern over his head, was the big man in whose pocket he had put the strychnine the afternoon Lute came. The man was in shirt sleeves and slippers, and he was scowling out into the night.

"What do you fellows want?" he asked roughly.

Frank said carelessly, "We're trying to catch one of our dogs that broke loose."

Saul started toward them. When he approached, the dog started to slink off. Saul caught sight of him and watched him disappear and then he came toward them.

"That looks like Bruce McIvor's dog," he said, hauling up before them. There was a hard suspicion in his face.

He looked at them both, especially at Frank, and then said curiously, quickly, "What's going on here, Nearing? Where's Bruce?"

Frank acted instantly, without thought. He stepped in and drove a smashing blow into Saul's jaw, putting all his solid big-boned weight behind it. The heavy muffled thud of it was distinct in the night, and then Saul went over backward, dropping the lantern. He fell on his back and did not move. Frank lunged for the lantern and extinguished it.

Lute whistled softly and looked down at Frank, who was kneeling by Saul. "Now what?" Lute asked.

Frank's head raised. Somebody was coming down the walk. He huddled there in the dark, motionless, until someone reached the corner and paused.

"Charlie," Frank called softly.

Charlie came over to them. He had a huge hunk of frozen moose meat in his hand as he stopped above Saul.

"He knew the dog," Frank explained, and came to his feet. "We've got to hide him until I get off in the plane."

"Hide him?" Lute echoed.

"You better hurry," Charlie said. "He'll freeze."

Frank whipped out his bandanna and knelt again by Saul and said, "Lift his head, someone." Lute raised Saul's head and Frank slipped the bandanna into Saul's mouth and tied it behind his head. It was an effective gag for Saul when he came to. The dog was forgotten now.

Frank came erect, his mind made up. "See anybody on the street, Charlie, when you came over?"

"Way down the street."

"All right, give me a hand, Lute. Get his arm around your shoulder."

He and Lute lifted Saul between them, each

taking an arm, and then Frank said, "Go out to the street, Charlie, and see if it's clear. First hang up that lantern on the fence. We'll be behind you. Whistle when it's all clear. Lute, we'll carry him over beside the hotel. Head for the shadows there, and hurry it."

"Where are you going to take him?" Lute asked.

"Hell, the hotel!" Frank said savagely. "We can't turn him loose and we can't let him freeze! Go ahead, Charlie."

Charlie went ahead out into the street, while Frank and Lute hugged the side of the café with Saul sagging between them. Charlie spent a long time searching the shadows up and down the street for any person abroad, and at last his low whistle came.

Saul's heavy body was dead weight, and Frank and Lute grunted under the load. They half ran, half walked across the road, swearing softly when they slipped under their awkward burden. It seemed an eternity to Frank before they reached the black shadows beside the log hotel. It was unsafe here, he knew, for at any moment Saul might rouse fighting, or a passer-by might spot them.

He left the others and went around the front corner of the hotel. Through the lobby windows he saw the night clerk in conversation with another man at the desk. Frank swore bleakly. They couldn't keep Saul, in shirt sleeves and slippers, out in this cold, nor could they lug him through the hotel lobby in plain sight of the clerk and his friend.

He looked up and down the street, couldn't see anybody, and then wheeled back to join Charlie and Lute.

"Charlie, there's a guy in there talking to the clerk. We've got to get them out of there, and do it quick. Go back to the woodpile and get a chunk of wood and chuck it through the window and run. Get a big one, so it'll make a racket."

Charlie vanished without a word. Frank leaned over to take Saul's arm, and he saw Saul's body stiffen under him. "Hurry it," he rapped out to Lute.

They heaved Saul up. He was fighting a little, as if drugged. And then the window in the rear crashed in a jangle of glass. Evidently Charlie's hunk of wood had sailed into the stove too, for there was a clatter of pots falling.

Frank and Lute, Saul between them, paused at the corner and looked through the window. The clerk, erect now, and the other man were both looking in the direction of the darkened dining room. Then the clerk walked out from behind the desk, a flashlight in his hand, and hurried into the dining room. The other man followed him, but went more slowly. They disappeared at last, and Frank opened the lobby door.

Panting and struggling with Saul, they hurried through the lobby and up the stairs. Saul was fighting half-heartedly now, trying to break away from them. On the stairs, he planted his feet against the steps and struggled.

"Lift his legs," Frank panted. Between them, carrying Saul in a sitting position, they struggled down the corridor to Frank's room. Saul was really fighting now, making low noises back of the gag, thrashing around and trying to free his arms. They set him down, and Frank pinned his arms behind him while Lute took Frank's key and opened the door.

Then Frank shoved him into the room, kicking the door shut behind him. He held Saul in the dark while Lute lighted the lamp. Saul wrestled silently.

"Listen!" Frank panted. "Are you going to stay still or will I have Lute hit you?"

Saul's struggles increased. He kicked back at Frank with his slippered feet, turning his shoulder with a great heaving strength.

Frank looked at Lute and nodded, and Lute swung. Again Saul took it on the chin. He sagged in Frank's arms, and Frank let him slide to the floor. Only then did he realize he was wringing wet with sweat, and that he was breathing as if he'd run a mile.

Frank sank on his knees and rolled Saul over. He felt gingerly of Saul's jaw, afraid that Lute might have broken it as it was pried open by the gag. But it seemed all right to him.

"One more thing, Lute," Frank said. "Go out and buy some tape. I'll sit on him till you get back."

Lute left, and Frank spent five minutes trussing

Saul's hands behind his back. Lute arrived with the tape, Frank ripped out the bandanna and taped Saul's mouth shut, and then the two of them hoisted him to the bed. He was just coming out of it when Frank finished running the cord from his duffel bag from Saul's wrists to the heavy iron bedstead.

Frank looked down at him and murmured, "You just ran into hard luck, fella. Nothing will happen to you if you take it easy."

Saul's eyes were hot with anger. He tried his bonds and found them tight. Then he tried to sit up, but the short length of rope wouldn't allow it. Sinking back onto the bed, he glared helplessly at them.

Lute said, "I better go help Charlie, hadn't I?"

It was the first time in ten minutes that Frank had thought of the dog. He was still loose, still the same threat. But if Saul broke loose, he would be even more dangerous than the dog. For a moment Frank was undecided, but he finally nodded to Lute, who went out.

Alone, Frank settled down into the chair and contemplated Saul. Everything had gone wrong that could go wrong, he reflected bitterly; everything that was left to chance, like a dog breaking loose or a man walking out with a lantern, went against him. He was like a man under a leaky roof in a driving rain, leaping from leak to leak, patching furiously, and as soon as one leak was stopped another would start. How long would it go on?

It was half an hour later that Charlie and Lute returned. Charlie had something heavy wrapped up in the sled tarp slung over his shoulder. He closed the door, swung the tarp to the floor, and let go the end. And out rolled the dog.

He came slowly to his feet, looking around him, and then slunk off into the farthest corner, baring his teeth in a silent snarl. Charlie threw him a hunk of moose meat, and then laughed at him. The dog had never been inside a building before, and he was too paralyzed with fear even to smell the meat.

Frank looked from the dog to Saul and shook his head. One more leak plugged, but what would the next one be? There was something wryly funny and fantastic in the scene in this room — a bully boy helpless on the bed, a sled dog in the corner, a broken window in the hotel kitchen, and coloring it all the long uncertain hours till noon tomorrow.

Lute said then, "Maybe it's none of my business, but you can't hold this man for five days until the plane goes, can you, Frank?"

Only then did Frank realize Lute didn't know why they had Saul. He explained about the search for Bruce that Kelcy had demanded, and that it was necessary to hold Saul only until the plane left tomorrow, lest he tell Millis and lead the search to Christmas Creek.

At the end of it, Lute only looked thoughtful. He said nothing.

146

Chapter Eleven

It was a little after twelve noon when Frank took the road out across the flats to where Kelcy McIvor and Corporal Millis, amid a crowd of youngsters, were standing on the bank watching the plane gas up. The white river was spotless, its new snow unbroken save for the two ski tracks that appeared from nowhere and laid their shallow channels to the shore. The sky was overcast, and now that the snow had stopped it was bitter cold.

Frank hauled up beside Millis, who was wearing a worn old buffalo coat and beaver cap. Millis greeted him unsmilingly; Kelcy nodded with the barest civility. She was wearing a long coat of matched black muskrat that made Frank, with his soiled parka and old beaver cap, feel shabby. Frank shucked his mitten and swiftly rolled a cigarette and lighted it. He contrived to look back over his shoulder toward the town. Nobody was coming. He had succeeded in keeping the maid out of his hotel room that morning, and right now Charlie and Lute, behind the locked door, were waiting for the sound of the plane's departure to walk out of the hotel and leave Saul and the dog for the frustrated chambermaid to discover.

A man was handing up the last of the five-gallon

cans of gasoline to the pilot on the wing of the old cabin job. It took only a few moments to finish the job, and then the pilot beckoned them over.

Only the pilot's seat and the one beside it had been left in the plane; all the other seats had been removed to provide cargo space. Immediately behind the pilot's seat was a bench bolted to the floor. Millis and Frank shared this, while Kelcy climbed in beside the pilot. He was a tall, blond, raffish-looking man with a pleasant grin. Once the plane took off and circled above Lobstick for height they leveled off and headed north. The drone of the motor was muffled enough to allow talk, but there was none. Millis hunched down in his coat, exchanged a few words with the pilot, and lapsed into silence. Frank had the uncomfortable feeling that he was on trial, beginning this moment. The few attempts by the pilot to engage Kelcy in conversation were futile. They sat like four contemplative hermits.

Frank watched the country below. Like all men who have traveled the bush and known its hardships, he was filled with an indefinable resentment against the plane. This was too easy; a man lost his perspective. Below them, the black spruce forest stretched out endlessly like clotted bird shot on white paper. The creeks and rivers and lakes were merely part of the background, blank spaces fringed with a gray smear of willows where the bird shot had not rolled. With a good trail and a light load he would take a week to do what this plane would accomplish in little better than an hour. It all ribboned out beneath him, that country he had traveled only a few days back, and none of it was recognizable, none of it was real.

The bitter chill of this high air crept into the plane, and Frank was glad of the sheep-lined overshoes he had bought. Millis looked miserable with the cold, and watching Kelcy's neck, Frank could see it quiver. She was shaking with the cold.

Frank said to Millis, "I could use this blanket we're sitting on."

"Take it, take it," Millis growled, and hoisted himself up. Frank pulled out the blanket, folded it, and handed it over to Kelcy. "If you'll wrap that around your feet it might help."

Kelcy looked at him, gratitude in her eyes, and thanked him stiffly. Millis was looking at him curiously, searchingly, and again Frank had the feeling he was on trial.

An hour or so later the pilot leaned back and said, "Where's this place on Horn Lake now?"

"Southwest shore, a mile or so east of the portage into Trimble Lake," Frank answered.

"You know this country pretty well," Millis remarked idly.

"I got around a bit last summer," Frank replied. He and Millis looked at each other a long second. This was one more fact Millis was filing away in his steel-trap memory.

The big white expanse of Horn Lake loomed

up ahead of them, barren and cold as death. The plane banked and lost altitude, and when it leveled off again the pilot had picked up the south shore of the lake and was following it.

Presently, in the arm of a small bay, they made out the clearing and snow-burdened shack of Weymarn just off the shore. A man was standing out in the snow before the shack waving at them. Frank saw Kelcy lean forward in her seat, and caught a glimpse of the breathless excitement in her face. But the distance was too great to tell whether or not it was Bruce.

Again the plane banked out toward the lake, and afterward sideslipped, losing altitude. It came into the narrow arm at the height of the treetops and settled into a long glide. Frank was a little excited in spite of himself. In a moment he would face Bruce. In the excitement and relief and anger that Bruce was sure to feel at sight of the three of them, would he blurt out what had happened and why? Frank tried to think of ways to silence him, and he could not. He'd have to use his judgment at the time, and if worse came to worse he could override him with the veiled threat of exposing his stealing of the letters.

The plane touched the snow in the middle of the arm and skimmed smoothly along until it lost speed. Then the motor opened up in a throaty roar as the pilot taxied in a half circle and brought the plane close to the shore.

The man waiting for them there was not Bruce; it was a middle-aged man, lean and unshaven and in need of a haircut. He followed the beaten path out to his water hole, and then waded out toward them through the snow. He was in shirt sleeves, but he didn't seem to mind the cold in his excitement. The pilot cut the switch, and in the following silence opened the door. He said to Kelcy, "Careful with that step."

They piled out into the snow, just as Weymarn reached them.

"Howdy," he said. "You folks in trouble?" He caught sight of Frank and said, "Hello, young feller," and came up and shook hands. Frank introduced him around. At the mention of Millis' title, Weymarn's face became wary.

"Where's Bruce?" Frank asked then.

Weymarn looked blank. "Bruce who?"

Frank's heart almost stopped beating. "Didn't Bruce McIvor come down from the height of land about four or five days ago?"

"Never heard of him," Weymarn said flatly. "Ain't nobody stopped by for a month, and then it was only a couple of Indians."

Frank turned his head to see Millis' accusing eyes on him, and then he looked at Kelcy.

"So you lied," Kelcy said quietly. "He never came over at all."

Frank turned to Weymarn, talking swiftly, desperately. "Look, about a week ago I left this man up at the head of Horn Creek. He had grub and snowshoes, and he couldn't have lost his way. You haven't seen him?"

Weymarn shook his head vigorously. "Two

weeks ago I come back from trippin' down north. But I ain't been gone more'n a half day from the shack since then. If he'd come while I was gone, I'd of saw his tracks, wouldn't I?"

Frank didn't answer. Nobody did. It was the silence of despair.

Weymarn suddenly shivered as a chill shook him. "Come up to the shack. You can't stand out here."

They followed him in silence. After cursing his dogs into silence, he apologized for the appearance of his shack and stood aside. Kelcy walked through the low door. It was the kind of place necessity had dictated, with only one window in the large main room and a dirt floor. An oil drum had been converted into a stove, and it gave out a welcome warmth. A crude hewn table, stump chairs, two double-deck bunks in the south wall, and a rack of groceries behind the stove were the only furnishings. A padlocked door opened onto a windowless room where Weymarn kept his trade goods and furs. A faint wild smell of fur mingled with the odor of grease and smoke that clung in the room. It was the home of a man who lived many heartbreaking portages away from civilization.

Entering, Frank wondered wildly if Weymarn might be lying. The thought was fantastic, but no more fantastic than the fact that Bruce wasn't there.

Weymarn and the pilot sensed that this was not their business and they sat behind the table, watching the others. Millis slipped off his heavy coat and then turned his back toward the stove. Kelcy sat on one of the stump chairs watching Frank, who was staring dazedly at almost everything in the room, seeking some clue to Bruce's presence.

Millis said matter-of-factly, "Well, Nearing, it's about time we got some truth into this business."

Frank's gaze whipped around. "I'm telling the truth, Millis, and you know it."

"Then where's Bruce?" Kelcy asked.

Frank shed his parka and let it drop to the floor. "Look." He squatted, picked up a sliver of wood from the untidy floor, and drew a straight line. "That's the Raft." He drew another straight line parallel to it. "That's the height of land north of Christmas Valley." He drew another straight line intersecting the second one at right angles. "That's Horn Creek." He drew a V at the end of that line. "That's this bay where we are." He jabbed his stick where Horn Creek met the height of land. "I left Bruce there exactly a week ago at a little after noon. He was on Horn Creek. He could have followed it if he was blind."

"Then where is he?" Millis asked roughly.

"I don't know." Frank hesitated. "To make sure he came this way instead of doubling back on our trail, I gave him a bare two days' grub. He might have headed back for Lobstick, but not without a gun. I know he didn't."

"Why did you give him only two days' food?" Kelcy asked angrily.

"I told you. So he'd come this way instead of following us."

"You mean you wanted him to come here?"

"Yes."

"Why?"

"It doesn't matter. I did," Frank said. "From the height of land to here it's an easy three days' travel. I did it last summer packing a heavy load uphill all the way. He could have crawled down here in three days."

"That's right," Weymarn put in.

A dog outside started to bark for no good reason, and afterward the silence ran on.

Millis said crisply then, "Well, he's not here. If you're telling the truth, Nearing, and left him up there, he's lost. Or something's happened to him. If he turned back to follow your trail, he's out in the bush on the other side of the height of land."

"And lost," Kelcy said accusingly. "Without a gun."

Frank came to his feet. "I left him at the height of land. I don't know where he is, but I want to look." He glanced over to the pilot. "Can you get down low enough for us to spot a trail?"

"It's against orders, but if Corporal Millis will assume the responsibility, I'll do it."

"Go warm her up," Millis said curtly.

The pilot rose and went out. Millis did not try to hide the suspicion with which he regarded Frank now as Frank slipped into his parka.

"There's some bloody funny business going on

154

here that you're going to have to explain, Nearing," Millis said.

"All right." Frank hesitated. "Am I under arrest?"

"For what?" Millis asked swiftly.

Frank said angrily, sardonically, "Are you trying to trap me into admitting I murdered him?"

"Did you?" Kelcy asked.

Frank put on his cap in disgust and tramped out. On the lake, the plane's motor coughed and started and sank into an even throaty roar. Frank walked out, shaking with anger. But behind that there was a small core of fear. Where was the kid? If anything had happened to him there was no question where the responsibility lay. Had he got just plain wild stubborn and decided, gun or no gun, that he'd drift back to Christmas Valley or Lobstick, trusting to his fool's luck to get him there?

Frank was in the plane when Kelcy and Millis and Weymarn trailed out. They waited a few minutes until the plane was warmed up, and then the pilot climbed in and they took off. Once in the air, they circled, and then Millis said curtly to Frank, "Tell him where to fly."

"There's a creek that empties into the head of this bay," Frank said. "Follow it up, and get down close enough so we can see something."

The pilot obeyed. Frank left his bench and sank on his knees and pressed his face to the glass of the cabin, looking down. Millis did too.

The land beneath them, a thick tangle of spruce

and poplar and birch, climbed toward the height of land. Frank watched it ribbon past, and he was puzzled. They were so low at times that game trails and even individual game tracks should have been visible, but the snow presented an unbroken and unmarked surface. Suddenly, Frank knew why, and he looked at Millis.

"There aren't any shadows today," he said. "We couldn't see his trail if it was a yard wide and six feet deep."

Millis said grimly, "We'll go on, just the same."

Once they reached the height of land Frank recognized the country. But across the open stretches where the three of them on snowshoes had tramped a good trail the snow was unmarked. Presently Millis grunted and looked at him. "Did you get this far?"

"We've passed where we left him," Frank said.

Millis said bluntly, "I think you're lying, Nearing. I don't think you were ever here a week ago. I don't think *he* was."

"And I don't either," Kelcy said.

Frank said brusquely to Millis, "Trade places with me. I'll prove it to you."

Frank knelt just behind the pilot then, and he studied the land a long time. Then he said to the pilot, "Can you swing around and head back and get a lot lower?"

Millis said, "Go ahead."

The plane wheeled and lost altitude. Frank tried desperately to remember this, but he couldn't. And then he saw the meadow where

156

Charlie had found the ashes of the old fire. "All right," Frank said. "When I tell you to circle, bank left."

The plane kept on. Frank was hunting for their last camp, but from here all the clusters of tamarack looked alike, and he didn't have the lie of the land to guide him. He said, "Swing to the right a little," and then on the heel of the words he thought he saw the camp and he said quickly, "Circle left!"

The wing tilted down, and the plane swung around. Then Frank said suddenly to Millis, "Look at that clearing in that tamarack! You can see fresh stumps in the dead stuff there." The plane came around more, and Frank continued: "When we get over that thicket to the right of them, look down. You'll see three poles slanting into the ground. That's where our tarp was."

The plane zoomed over the spot, and it seemed to Frank they were barely skimming the treetops. But for one fleeting instant they looked down onto the old camp site. The snow had drifted over the brush and the fire, but there the three poles were. Frank looked up at Millis.

"All right," Millis said to the pilot. "Let's head back for Weymarn's."

They landed on the lake in front of the shack in the lowering dusk. Weymarn met them again, and they climbed silently out of the plane. Frank walked straight up to Weymarn.

"Weymarn, do you mind lending your dogs for a few days?"

Millis came up behind Frank, and Weymarn said, "Take 'em. You see him up there?"

Frank said in a meager voice, "No, not a sign of him." His glance shuttled to Millis. "You never answered me when I asked you if I was under arrest."

"Why do you want to know?"

"If I'm not, I'm going to take Weymarn's dogs and find Bruce. He's between here and the height of land."

Millis looked at him a long time, and then he glanced at Kelcy, who was standing beside him. Frank waited for his answer, but Millis kept looking at the shore, his eyes musing. Suddenly Millis murmured. "How are you fixed for beds, Weymarn?"

"Plenty. Hell, I got a roomful of point blankets in there you can use. You figure to stay over?"

Millis nodded and glanced at Frank. "I always give a man a chance," he said mildly. "Sure, go look. I'll go with you."

"And so will I," Kelcy said.

But Kelcy didn't go with them. That night after supper she argued bitterly and interminably with Millis, who was adamant. The plane was going out tomorrow and would call for them in five days. Millis wanted Kelcy to go out with the pilot. Kelcy not only refused, but insisted that she accompany Frank and Millis on the search for Bruce. The compromise was reached long after Frank had rolled into the new blankets from Weymarn's supply on the dirt floor beside the stove. Kelcy would stay here with Weymarn and wait for them.

When the lamp was finally blown and the five of them settled into silence, Frank lay awake staring at the small glimmer of light that played on the roof from the stove. This was trouble, real trouble, and there was no use denying it. Where was the kid? In these long dismal hours since dark fell that question had been haunting him. Try as he might, he couldn't believe that Bruce had doubled back and followed their trail to the Raft. A bushman could sum up his chances on making it, and then bull it through with only snowshoes and a blanket — and a gun. But Bruce wasn't made of that tough stuff, and he didn't have a rifle. Then if he didn't turn south, he must have headed down Horn Creek and lost his way. But he couldn't lose it, he just couldn't! And then Frank had made the full circle: If Bruce hadn't turned back and he hadn't lost his way, where was he?

Kelcy had refused to talk to him that evening, and Millis had treated him with the same impersonal courtesy he would extend to a man about to be hanged. Only Weymarn, probably because of a bushman's ingrained antagonism for the law, treated him as if he weren't already a condemned man. Which he was, if he didn't find Bruce, he thought somberly. It wasn't a comforting thought to sleep on.

Next morning, while the pilot in the cold dawn was burning his fire pot under the canvas hood looped over the plane's engine to warm it up for the day's flight, Frank and Millis left the shack.

Millis no longer looked like a policeman. He was dressed in a worn and shabby bush outfit borrowed from Weymarn, but underneath the ragged parka was strapped his pistol. It was the only gun they carried. For dog feed they loaded dried whitefish from Weymarn's supply into the sled, and by daylight they were gone.

Years of town living and an occasional patrol on which he saw everything from the warm cariole of a driven toboggan had not improved Millis' physical condition. He and Frank took turn about breaking trail, and at the first night's camp Millis fell asleep while they were waiting for the kettle to boil.

The second day of facing the same upgrade without Weymarn's hunting trails to follow was agony to Millis. When Frank was breaking trail he set a long easy tireless pace that left Millis far behind and wild with anger at his inability to get work out of this strange team of dogs. But when Frank was driving, the dogs crowded right behind Millis, sometimes stepping on his shoes and tripping him. But he was a stubborn man and he did not complain, although that second night he felt burned out and gutted with exhaustion.

The following day they were nearing the height of land, and the spruce forest was thinning out for an occasional muskeg and jack-pine ridge.

Horn Creek had shrunk until now they could step across it. Millis was plodding ahead on the shoes, Frank driving. Occasionally Frank would leave the trail, cross the creek, and cast about for any sign of drifted snowshoe tracks, since the overcast sky again washed out the shadows. It was after one of these forays that he returned to the team and noted a change in the dogs. Gone was their tongue-out, tail-wagging impatience to go ahead. Their ears were erect, their heads lifted a little as they keened the wind, and their tails were not wagging. Frank spoke to them, and they settled into their collars reluctantly, hesitantly.

Millis was already out of sight in a stand of scrub balsam ahead. Frank mushed the dogs on, but he knew they were uneasy. They kept looking from side to side, and the leader moved with an alert caution.

Presently, just before Millis' trail dived into the balsam thicket, the dogs stopped. The leader's ears went down; he turned his head to look at Frank, and then he circled out in the snow, trying to turn back. Frank spoke sharply to him. The dog lay down in the snow, waiting for his trimming for refusing to go ahead.

Frank glanced ahead at the balsam thicket, puzzled. Millis was up there, and should have seen what panicked the dogs. Frank turned the sled on its side, and as a further precaution against the dogs' bolting he tied the tail rope to a tree.

Then he went on into the thicket. Scrub balsam can grow as thick as a hedge, but there was a break in this where Millis had naturally sought a trail. Frank followed his tracks deep into the thicket, and presently it broke away for an up-thrust of rock. The trees bordering the opening had died and their gray skeletons stood erect around the small clearing.

Frank looked around the clearing and then ahead to Millis' trail. And then he looked again at the clearing, his attention caught by a lagging impression.

There, on the border of the thicket where they blended with the dead trees, was a pair of snow-shoes thrust erect in the snow.

Frank's gaze shifted to a hump in the snow, and he knew they had come to the end of the trail.

That hump under the snow was Bruce McIvor.

Chapter Twelve

Frank lifted his voice and called, "Millis!" and whistled sharply three times. He did not move out of his tracks, only gazed at the hump in the unbroken snow in blank and wry bewilderment.

It was a long minute before Millis, red-faced with exertion, came back into the clearing. He looked sharply, curiously at Frank, who gestured, silent, toward the hump.

"There are his shoes. And there he is."

Millis silently regarded the hump. A long minute afterward his glance lifted to Frank. "You didn't have a hard time finding him, did you?" he asked in a thin voice.

"The dogs wouldn't come into this balsam. I came on ahead to see why," Frank explained patiently, a faint anger edging his voice. He looked levelly at Millis, who was regarding him with searching scrutiny.

Millis said then, "You stay there."

Millis toed out of his shoes and waded up to the hump. He knelt then, and with his mittened hand he scraped away the snow on the top of the hump. A khaki-colored shoulder was revealed to him. He straightened slowly and stared at the body, not saying anything. Then he clipped out, "Build a fire out there on the trail. Don't come any closer than you are."

Frank hastily built a fire, watching Millis, wondering bleakly if Bruce had starved to death. With his snowshoes, Millis labored mightily to clear away the snow in a ten-foot circle around Bruce. And as he worked, the whole scene slowly took shape under Frank's curious and dismal gaze. The packsack, the cup, and the kettle, all were uncovered. The bannock was gone, stolen by squirrels. Millis left things as he found them, until the whole scene was laid bare. Bruce had fallen across the fire face down, where he still lay. Millis studied his attitude, photographing it in his mind, and then he said to Frank, "Go get the ax."

When Frank returned with the ax he had just reached the fire when Millis said, "Don't come any closer. Throw it."

Frank did. With the ax, Millis chopped away the ice that was holding Bruce's parka to the ground. Finished, he rolled Bruce over. He came stiffly, sickeningly over on his back, frozen in an attitude of sleep, both hands raised even with his face, right knee a little bent.

Millis stared at that face a long time. Frank could see its bluish tinge, like the face of a man who has died of asphyxiation. Millis said quietly, "You can come over now."

Frank came slowly into the clearing, looking at Bruce with a kind of dread fascination. Bruce's parka was burned on the chest and side clear down to the skin.

Millis looked obliquely at Frank. "Recognize

164

it? The way he died, I mean?"

"No."

"Strychnine."

Frank's gaze whipped up swiftly to Millis' face, and he could not keep the surprise out of his eyes. "Are you sure?"

"This is the second one of these I've seen," Millis said grimly. "A breed up on Shore Lake killed his wife this way five years ago."

Into Frank's stunned mind came the memory of that bottle of strychnine back in the shack on Christmas Creek. Had some of it got in Bruce's food? He rejected that immediately as impossible.

Millis said quietly, "We hanged him."

Frank roused and said blankly, "What?"

"We hanged him — the Indian." He had never ceased watching Frank and now he asked abruptly, "Where'd you get the strychnine, Nearing?"

"You think I poisoned him?" Frank asked harshly.

"Where did his food come from?"

"From us, from the same lot of stuff that we've been eating out of for two months!" Frank said hotly.

Millis came back to his other question. "Where'd the strychnine come from?"

Frank's mouth was open to tell him, and then he remembered Kelcy. If he told about the strychnine, then the whole sordid story that Kelcy had so bravely tried to hide would be laid bare. A warning voice told Frank this was no time for the niceties; he was being accused of murder. But the stubborn pride in him spoke louder. If Millis was ever to know about the strychnine, it would not be from him. Kelcy's suspicion of him and Lute didn't count now, for it was too late for Millis to snoop and hurt them. It wasn't that at all; it was pride and a hatred of being a squealer — and something else that Frank couldn't put in words.

He said, "I don't know," and shook his head.

Millis said doggedly, "You gave him his food and he ate it and now he's dead. You wouldn't tell us where he was until you were crowded into it, and even now you won't tell us why you brought him over here." He said softly, "Nearing, you're a quiet devil and I've not held that against you. But when this is told to a jury that tries you, you'll hang, man! Can't you see that?"

"I didn't kill him!" Frank said bitterly, hotly. "That's all that counts, Millis. I didn't kill him!"

"Can you prove it?"

Frank got a grip on his temper and forced his mind into a semblance of alertness. He took a deep breath and looked at Bruce dispassionately, trying to bring some logic into this. His food wasn't poisoned, Frank was certain. Yet it was strychnine that killed him, and that strychnine had been within reach of Bruce.

He said quietly, "Have you searched him?"

"Meaning you think he might have committed suicide?"

"I don't know!" Frank said savagely. "Why

don't you do your job instead of trying to hang a man without a hearing?"

Millis' broad face flushed under that thrust, and he knelt beside Bruce. One parka pocket was burned out. The other held a tobacco pouch. His other pockets held a miscellany of coins and .22 shells and matches and nails. There was nothing. To get to his hip pockets, Millis gingerly rolled him back in the original position. There were two handkerchiefs in his hip pockets.

But Frank thought of something. He said, "Did you look in the fire? Whatever was in that parka pocket either burned or is in the fire."

Again Millis rolled Bruce over, and then stirred in the ashes of the fire. A shred of cloth ribboned out of the fringe of ashes.

"His sugar sack," Frank pointed out.

Millis didn't hear him. He'd found something buried in the thin ashes at the edge of the fire. It was a small bottle with a scorched cork. Millis wiped away the ashes from the glass and inside he could see a powder faintly scorched from the heat. He looked up at Frank, who held out his hand for the bottle. Frank examined it, sure that this was Joe McKenzie's bottle, and handed it back. "It's half gone," he pointed out, his voice wry with angry relief.

Millis didn't answer. He simply stared at the bottle, turning it over and over in his hand, as if he doubted its existence, and his broad face reflected a bewilderment that Frank shared.

Millis said gently, "Would a man wanting to

commit suicide put strychnine in his tea, cork the bottle, and put it back in his pocket again?" He slowly lifted his gaze to Frank.

"No, but he might throw it in the fire."

"True."

There was a long silence, and Millis still held the bottle in his hand. His fist folded over it, and he stared thoughtfully at Bruce. He asked gently, "You gave him bannock, you say?"

"Yes." Frank was following Millis' train of thought now. "If it had been poisoned, this place would be littered with dead squirrels and chipmunks."

"And you gave him sugar?"

"That's part of the sack you pulled out of the fire."

Millis slowly pocketed the bottle. He looked squarely at Frank then and said, "A no-good kid is taken seven days away from home, sits down to boil tea, and suddenly decides to take his life. I don't believe it."

Frank's green eyes glinted coldly. "Maybe you believe this, then: I took him out here and left him poisoned food and came back to Lobstick and admitted to you where he was. I brought you up here, and I even found him for you so I could prove what?"

"That he's dead but you didn't kill him."

Frank shook his head. "Nights are dark and shells are cheap, Millis. And that way is easier, isn't it?"

"Still, he's dead, isn't he?"

"And I killed him?"

Millis shook his head slowly. "The evidence says maybe. I say maybe. We'll see what time says."

Their gruesome burden wrapped tightly in the tarpaulin, they pulled into Weymarn's three days later long after dark. Because there were no dogs staked out to warn of their approach, they hauled up where the lake trail climbed to the shack and were not seen. Frank had been breaking trail, and at each breathing spell he had waited for a hint from Millis as to how he was going to break the news to Kelcy. But it never came, and this was his last chance.

He stopped the dogs and swung out of the trail and tramped back to Millis. "You go ahead," he said.

"Can't face the music, eh?" Millis growled.

Frank couldn't see his face in the dark, but he could judge from his tone of voice that Millis hated the job that was facing him and that he was hiding his hatred behind surliness.

"No," Frank admitted honestly. "She's thought I killed him all along. She — won't want to see me."

Millis took a deep breath. "All right. You stay outside."

He mushed the dogs and they pulled up into the yard beside the shack. The one small window laid its square of lamplight out on the snow, making this scene as lonely-looking as a cold star.

Weymarn had heard the sled pull in and he opened the door. Millis spoke to him in the door-way and Weymarn stepped out into the night and Millis went inside.

Frank and Weymarn met by the sled.

"So you found him," Weymarn said in a hushed voice. Frank nodded and they stood side by side peering down at the tarp-wrapped bulkiness in the sled.

Weymarn said softly, excitedly, "Frank, if you want to make a break for it, now's the time! I'll help you unload him and you take the team! That plane ain't due till nine tomorrow. You'd have all night for a head start."

"Thanks," Frank said. "I guess not."

Even Weymarn thought he was guilty and Weymarn knew less about it than anyone. If he thought so, Frank could imagine what Kelcy thought. He wondered how she would take the news of her brother's death. She was a strong girl, a sensible one too, and Frank had a shrewd idea that deep within her Kelcy had prepared herself for just this thing. If she would turn on him and curse him and blame him in one wild torrent of grief and anger, it wouldn't be so bad. But he suspected that Kelcy could be quick to anger and sharp of tongue in small things, but in the bigger things she would not. She would just hate him, that's all — hate him with all the deep quiet strength of her.

Frank said dismally, "Where can we put him, Weymarn?"

Weymarn was silent a moment, and then he said, "On the meat cache, I reckon. He's wrapped agin' the whisky jacks and such, ain't he?"

Frank said he was. He unlashed the load, and then they lifted the stiff unyielding burden out of the sled. The meat cache was behind the shack and to the side, a bare pole rack up on forked posts about head high, designed to keep the meat away from the dogs.

Afterward they unhooked the dogs and chained them out and fed them, and still Millis did not come out. Frank's reluctance to go in had been communicated to Weymarn now. He stood beside Frank, hands in pockets, shivering under his shirt in the sharp cold.

Frank said, "Go on in, Weymarn, and break it up. It'll have to come sometime."

"Sure," Weymarn said. He went inside reluctantly. Frank reached in his pocket for his tobacco pouch and rolled a smoke quickly. He might as well go in now; he'd have to face it sooner or later.

He lighted his cigarette, donned his mittens, and pushed away from the wall. And then the door opened and Kelcy stepped out and closed the door behind her. Frank dropped his cigarette and waited.

Kelcy walked slowly over to him and paused in front of him.

"I don't think you did it, Frank," she said softly. "I — It's too horrible!"

Frank was speechless. He stood there awk-

171

wardly, fumbling in his mind for some speech of condolence, but none would come.

"It's better this way," Kelcy went on miserably. "He was so weak — so terribly weak."

Frank murmured, "There's nothing so bad about dying when it's that hard to live."

Kelcy said, "Was it suicide, Frank?"

"Either that or he got it by mistake. It couldn't be any other way, because I didn't poison him."

"And the strychnine? How could he get it?"

Frank shook his head. "It's Joe McKenzie's bottle. Bruce stole it from my place."

"Then he must have intended to commit suicide," Kelcy said. "Doesn't that prove it?"

"Or he wanted to destroy the evidence I held against him."

"Then why didn't he just throw it away?"

"I don't know."

They looked at each other in the darkness. It was a strange conversation to Frank, almost unreal. This girl, his enemy, he had thought, was defending him now, making out his case for him.

"You didn't tell Millis you had the strychnine, did you?" Kelcy asked abruptly.

"No."

"Why not?"

Frank shrugged, faintly embarrassed. "I don't know. He'd jump McKenzie and the breed would tell. Bruce is dead. What I knew about him doesn't matter now." He hesitated. "Maybe that's sentiment. I don't know. Part of it's pride, I suppose.

I was going to let you say whatever had to be said."

"And that is nothing, nothing!" Kelcy said passionately. "So long as you aren't harmed, Frank, do we have to tell Millis anything about Bruce?"

"No."

"I'm thinking of Dad," Kelcy said, almost fiercely. "He's earned that much consideration from me, from everyone! To him Bruce was a lovable, headstrong misfit, but not bad. And Dad is old, Frank. He never knew. He won't ever have to know, will he?"

"No," Frank said, his voice reassuring.

Kelcy sighed. "I've been wrong about you. I never understood your unfriendliness, and I'm afraid I still don't. But I know something about you now — just one thing. You could have helped yourself by telling Millis about Bruce, about his strychnine peddling, and you didn't."

"I could have kept quiet because of our bargain," Frank murmured. "Did you think about that?"

"I thought about it, but somehow I don't think that was your reason."

She hesitated, as if she were going to say more, and Frank waited. And he was suddenly aware that she was crying — silently, fighting it, not admitting her grief.

And Frank did what pity would make any man do; he put out his arms and she came into them, and hiding her face in his old parka, she let grief take her.

Chapter Thirteen

The plane came into Lobstick a little after midday out of a cold raw wind. Before the curious had time to gather, Millis and Frank and Kelcy crossed the flats and parted on the street, Millis and Kelcy seeking her father, and Frank free to do what he liked. He was not under arrest, but Millis had warned him frankly that he was liable to be at any moment. He could not leave town, but outside of that he was at liberty.

Frank sought the hotel, hunching against the wind that was not a clean cold but that seemed to have the bleak and clammy chill of a wet, deep, sunless pit about it. It was a day for death, Frank thought somberly, thinking of Kelcy and Millis and Kelcy's father. Even the thought that yesterday his letter had gone to the recorder did not cheer him at the moment.

At the hotel he got a room. Wondering if Charlie and Lute had returned from the trip up the Wailing to get Bruce's dogs, he inquired after them and was told they were registered.

Upstairs, he knocked on Charlie's door, and a sleepy voice answered him. Charlie was surprised at the sight of him; he had been drowsing on the bed, and hadn't heard the plane come. A moment later Lute came in, and he was carrying a bottle of whisky under his arm. He had heard Frank's voice from the room next door. A recent shave had given him that clean fresh look again, and he seemed pleased and almost boyishly excited to see Frank. Critically, Frank noticed that bush life had leaned Lute down a little, but his shoulders under his woolen shirt were still thick and powerful.

Without a word Frank took the bottle and poured himself a drink and downed it. The raw heat of it made him shiver pleasurably.

Charlie said from the bed, "What's happened to you, Frank?"

Frank set the bottle down gently and announced, "Bruce was found dead two miles after we left him, Charlie. Strychnine poisoning."

Quick attention came into Charlie's dark eyes, but he said nothing, after his fashion. It was Lute who echoed blankly, "Poisoned? How could that happen?"

Frank sank into a chair and thrust his feet forward. "Lute, you remember that bottle of strychnine I put on the bookshelf that night Bruce drifted in?"

"Sure. The bottle you took, you mean?"

"Took?"

Lute's solid face settled into a frown, changing the bold planes of it. "Didn't you? It wasn't there that day you left. I know, because that evening I read *Don Quixote* again. When I reached for the book I missed the bottle."

"Bruce stole it," Frank said. He told them of

175

finding Bruce, of Millis' accusation, of the finding of the bottle, and of Millis' reluctant conclusion that Bruce's death resulted from accident or suicide. He also told of Kelcy's talk with him, but this he glossed over for a reason that was obscure to him. It was private, and no words could convey either the mood of that hour or the surprise it had held for him. Lute and Charlie listened with rapt attention as Frank cheerlessly admitted that Millis still didn't know why Bruce was taken there.

"And he won't know — not for another week," Frank said grimly. "I'm telling nothing until I get the confirmation of that claim from Resource."

The recounting of the story filled him with a distaste and foreboding and he got up to pour another drink.

Charlie had rolled a cigarette, and now he snapped a match alight and touched it to the cigarette and carefully put the match out, breaking it in his brown fingers from long bush habit.

"I never thought McIvor would do that," Charlie remarked then.

"I'm with you," Lute agreed in a slow puzzled voice.

"Well, he did it, and it wasn't an accident," Frank said.

"But he could have spilled some in his pocket and not known it," Lute said, and then added, "or could he? No, I don't suppose he could. He'd have known, then, and been careful." He looked at Frank and asked idly, "I suppose the cork was burned and the bottle cracked, and the stuff was destroyed."

"No. That's why I'm sure it was suicide," Frank said. "The bottle wasn't destroyed. He'd thrown it at the fire, and it rolled out. The cork was charred but it's still in the bottle with half the strychnine behind it."

"Still?" Lute asked. "You have the bottle with you, then?"

"No. Millis will send it off for routine analysis. It's exhibit A, the death weapon," and Frank made a wry face.

Charlie started probing then. Lute listened to their conversation but took no part in it. His chair was tilted back against the wall, his arms folded over his chest, and his pale eyes at times were almost dreamy.

Frank was in the middle of an explanation when his voice died off, and he tilted his head, as if listening. There was a faint rumble of tramping feet downstairs. Then he turned back to Charlie and resumed the explanation.

Minutes later there was a knock on the door, which Lute answered. Frank couldn't see the man, but he heard him speak.

"Is Nearing in there? If he is, you better tell him to get the hell out of here right away! There's a bunch of bums downstairs lookin' for him."

Frank went to the door and hauled it open and said, "Who are they?"

The agitated clerk said angrily, "Hell, I don't know! Everybody. The bull cook is standing there on the stairs with a meat cleaver. You better beat it, Nearing!"

Frank pushed past him and headed for the stairs. When he made the turn in them, he saw the cook, cleaver in hand, holding at bay a couple of dozen men clotted arguing around the foot of the stairs. At sight of Frank the talk faded off. Frank said, "Anybody want to see me?"

The group stirred at its outer edge, and a bold voice rose above the angry babble to say, "Yeah, I do," and then Saul Chenard stepped out. His mackinaw was open over his big bull chest and his soft, full-lipped mouth was twisted in a sneer.

Frank looked at him closely and murmured, "You like your own odds, don't you, when you get even?"

"Hell with gettin' even!" Saul said harshly. "I don't count the other night. We aren't here for that, Nearing, and you know it!"

Frank looked with a new curiosity at the men. These men were ugly, and they were listening to every word Saul spoke for them.

"What do you want, then?"

"Bruce McIvor had a lot of friends around this town," Saul said bluntly. "Every one of 'em is wonderin' how you could take Millis up to the body, and then say you didn't poison him."

Frank's lip curled at the corner. "Go back and ask Millis if I'm under arrest," he said curtly. "If he says yes, I'll go with you. If he says no, stay away from me."

A man in the rear shouted, "We know murder

178

as good as Millis does!"

Saul had been covertly watching the cook, who turned now to look at Frank. Saul dived at the cook, wrapped his arms around him, and threw him back into the press of men, who grabbed him to disarm him. Two of the bolder spirits broke past Saul and grabbed at Frank.

Lute and Charlie had been standing silently on the step behind Frank. It was Lute who sailed past Frank and lunged into the two men, bowling them down into their companions.

Saul made a lunge for Frank and Frank hit him in the face, and then the battle was on. Charlie picked up the handiest chair and, swinging it like an ax, moved forward into the press of the snarl.

From the steps the clerk bayed shrilly for them to stop, but nobody heard him. There were two distinct clots in that lobby. One of them was around Lute, who stood spraddle-legged, a man on his back, and fought and kicked with a grunting viciousness as they closed on him. Charlie was backing a half-dozen men into a wider circle with his swinging chair, while behind him Frank was trying to break away from Saul, who had him pinned against the wall and was driving great grunting blows into his body.

Frank bent his knees a little, and when his shoulder was against Saul's head he raised it. As Saul's face came up he sent a looping blow into it that mashed the corner of Saul's lip against his teeth and went slithering off the side of his face, greased with new blood.

Saul swung wildly at him and lunged for his body, and this time Frank met him, shoulder to shoulder, with an impact that jarred him clear down to his ankles. It was a blind, clubbing sideswipe with his fist that Saul used then, with no direction, no skill. He missed his first blow and his arm hooked around Frank's neck, and Frank brought his elbow into Saul's midriff with a savage lift that drove every breath of air from Saul's lungs. His arm locked around Frank's head, gagging for breath, Saul tried to wrench Frank off his feet, and the great power in his shoulders made Frank's neck crack. He clawed futilely at Saul's chest, his head twisting ever higher, and then in panic desperation he stomped on Saul's feet.

The hold broke, and with his foot braced against the wall Frank lowered his head and hit Saul in the body with every ounce of strength he had, sending him back into the others.

Out of the corner of his eye he saw a chair slide across the floor and catch Charlie from behind, and Charlie went down. Eight or ten men boiled over him at Frank, and Frank met them swinging, his back to the wall. It was a brief moment of wild rage that sustained him as he slogged murderously at faces, any faces, and then a blow caught him in the stomach and paralyzed him and seemed to freeze his arms in mid-air. He went down, down, and his face hit the rough floor, and some instinct brought his arms to his chest and his knees up to shield himself against the awkward stomping kicks. He gagged then for breath, and he did not hear the gunshot.

It was Millis, brown tunic unbuttoned, service revolver in hand. He was in that mob, slugging with his gun, before he bawled, "Break it up! Break it up!"

He shoved and pushed men aside until he came to the clot of men over Frank and he dove into them shoulder first, low, bowling them away and going down with them as they fell. He came to his feet and stood over Frank, and once more he raised his gun and shot into the roof three times.

It was the near bellow of that gun in the packed room that calmed them. And once he had their attention, Millis acted. He swung his gun like a whip, moving forward, cursing, kicking, slashing anything that stood in front of him, and finally the men broke in a panic for the door. Save for the men on the floor, the lobby was soon empty. The clerk ran down from the steps and locked the door.

Millis, breathing deeply, turned to view the damage. The room was wrecked, the couch and chairs overturned, the contents of spittoons and ash trays smeared across the floor, the deal desk on its side. A moose head, one antler wrenched off, lay absurdly on the floor, nose to a crack, glass eyes wide and unblinking and alarmed-looking.

One man got to his feet and Millis booted him roughly toward the door. Lute was sitting against the wall, feeling his jaw gently, a man lying across his knees. One man was really hurt, the skin peeled off his scalp, which was bleeding freely. Charlie was erect, grimacing as he tried to stretch out his leg. Millis said to the clerk, "Get that man to the doctor, and do it quick!" and didn't wait to see if he was obeyed.

He came over to Frank, who was standing now, weaving a little on his feet. Frank's shirt was torn to ribbons, and a great bloody scratch ran the length of his bare arm. One cheekbone was red, oddly out of shape, and a corner of his mouth was puffed out. His right ear was red as blood, and the smoldering anger in his green eyes had not died yet when Millis confronted him.

"All right?" Millis asked.

Frank nodded.

Millis cursed then, and turned to regard the clerk and the cook, carrying out the hurt man, with a baleful look.

"What started it?" he asked Frank.

"The mob down here wanted to talk to me. They accused me of Bruce's murder, and piled into the cook, and then the fight was on." He said less swiftly, "Thanks. I was in a tough spot."

Charlie and Lute limped up. Lute had one eye swollen shut, and his knuckles were like raw beef. Charlie walked with a limp, but was otherwise unmarked, for they had ignored him.

Millis regarded the pair of them and his gaze shifted to Frank. "You're collecting again for that damned sour way of yours, Nearing!"

Frank didn't say anything.

Millis drew a great breath and buttoned his coat. His holster was not on him, and he rammed his gun into the waistband of his breeches.

"Well, you're not safe around here," he said grimly. "Damned if I'll run up to Wailing River every time I want to talk to you, either. You better come with me."

"Is this an arrest, Millis?" Frank demanded.

"Call it anything you like!" Millis said savagely. "God almighty, I've got the murder of a girl on my hands, and then this poisoning and now I've got to wet-nurse you!"

Frank didn't answer and the anger died in Millis' pale eyes. "All right," he said resignedly. "Call it protective custody. I won't lock you up, but I don't want you on the street. You can use our spare bedroom."

He looked balefully at Charlie and Lute. "You two better stay here and keep off the streets, too." He hesitated and then said briefly, with a depthless, passionate, harried disgust, "Oh, hell."

That night after supper Lute stepped into Millis' office and hesitated inside.

"Come in, come in," Millis said testily. "This is a public office."

"I'd like to see Frank if I can," Lute said.

Millis pointed toward a door in the side wall. "There's a back stairs in that hall. Back bedroom."

Lute thanked him and went on up. He found

Frank in a small, sparsely furnished room under the eaves. It was a girl child's room, papered with a gay flower design, its curtains of chintz, and on the low dressing table against the wall was an oversize Teddy bear with a blue ribbon on its throat.

Lute stepped into the room, looked about him, and grinned. Frank was half sitting, half lying on the bed, his shirt off, his underwear top dirty and torn.

"Nice place," Lute remarked. "A little floozy for my taste, but good."

Frank grinned sheepishly. "Millis has got a daughter outside at school. Guess what I wore at dinner tonight."

"I couldn't."

"A shirt with a boiled front and no collar. It's all Millis had."

Lute laughed. "I'll bring you some clothes to-morrow." He sank onto a rickety chair. "Can you go out?"

"After dark, Millis says."

Again Lute grinned at the picture of Frank in this room, and Frank rolled a smoke. They talked of the fight and Lute reported Charlie had a badly wrenched knee. His own left eye was almost swollen shut and was taking on a nice red color.

Presently he pulled out an opened letter and handed it to Frank. "This was what I was going to show you this afternoon when the trouble started. It came in the mail while you were away."

Frank took the letter out and opened it.

Dear Lute:
Phillips sent this word in today by a messenger. In his last mail received at the Force Lake camp there's a letter from Jean's lawyer saying he'll be hauled into court when he returns. They've traced his connection with you, and he'll have to tell your whereabouts or take a stiff fine. I suggest you clear out of there in a hurry. Joe is coming down week after next, so you'd better make it by then. Regards and luck,

CARL

Frank read it twice and looked up at Lute.
"Jean's my former wife," Lute said.
"And Carl?"
"My lawyer. I met Joe through him."
Frank folded the letter slowly and murmured, "Want your money back, Lute?"
Lute shook his head. "No. But I wondered if you wanted the other thousand I promised you."
"Do you need it?"
Lute nodded. "That's all I brought along, that thousand and some pocket money. Now that I've got to move, I'll need it to get settled somewhere else. I can write to my partner, but it's dangerous." He paused. "You'll get the money. You've kept your word. And of course, you don't have to agree to this; nobody's making you."
Frank smiled faintly, his curious gaze on Lute.

185

"In some ways, you're a kid, Lute. What's to stop me right now from demanding ten thousand dollars from you? Would you pay it, rather than face your wife?"

Lute looked disturbed. "Why, yes, I suppose."

Frank grinned. "Well, I'm not doing it. And you pay off that other thousand when it's safe to get it."

"Thanks," Lute said.

"When will you go?"

"Next plane, I think. After that, it wouldn't be safe to stay."

Frank was watching him curiously, and said suddenly, "I misjudged you, Lute. I thought your story was a gag."

"I know you did," Lute said, and he grinned too. He rose and Frank handed him his letter.

"We've been over some jumps," Frank said thoughtfully. "I've been a pretty tough cookie at times, Lute. I guess you know why."

Lute nodded and smiled. "All is forgiven."

"Going up to the shack?"

Lute nodded. "After the funeral tomorrow I'll go and get my things. That is, if I can borrow the dogs. It'll have to be a fast trip, too."

"You're welcome to them," Frank said.

Lute picked up his cap. "I'll bring your clothes over tomorrow, Frank. Sweet dreams in your baby-blue bedroom."

He went out. Downstairs he bade a polite good night to Millis. Outside he headed for the hotel. He was smiling in the dark. Frank had swallowed it, bait, hook, line and sinker, and with not a flicker of suspicion.

If Millis was going to send the strychnine — no, flour — out for analysis, it would go on the next plane. And on that same plane he would fly out. By the time the hue and cry was raised after him, he would be hidden outside, away from this trap. That letter, which he had sent the supper hour composing in his room, had done the trick. Frank hadn't looked at the smeared postmark on the envelope which was the envelope of the letter Bruce had opened.

All in all he considered himself in luck. There was one more job that might be necessary, but that would be as easy as the others. He was a little annoyed that they'd found Bruce. He hadn't counted on that, but he was taking care of it.

Chapter Fourteen

Saul was one of the first to fade out of the hotel lobby at Millis' entrance. He had courage, but it was tempered with discretion, and his recipe for survival included the belief that only fools argue with policemen. Besides, Frank was taken care of. Saul had seen him go down in that fighting, kicking mob, and he considered the score even.

He was holding a handkerchief to the mashed corner of his mouth as he came into the restaurant, Bonnie trailing after him. Like everybody else within a radius of two hundred yards of the hotel, she had heard the racket and had watched part of the fight.

Upstairs, she said, "Sit down, Saul, and let me look at it."

"It's nothing," Saul replied. All the same, he sat on the edge of the bed in her room and let her look at it, and then make a fuss over him. The skin on his cheek was torn where Frank's fist had raked along his face, and three of his teeth had been loosened. But he felt a quiet exhilaration as he told Bonnie what had happened over there.

When she was finished, he stood up and regarded himself in the mirror. A small strip of tape at the corner of his mouth hid the mark. He rolled up his sleeves and poured some water into the crockery washbowl.

Bonnie, sitting on the bed, said, "All the same, Saul, you were taking a chance."

"Why? I was Bruce's closest friend. That's where I belonged, in the front of the fight."

Bonnie said flatly, "You didn't belong in it at all. Bruce is dead. We're safe. Stay out of the whole mess from now on."

Saul soaped his hands and spoke reasonably. "How would that look? Me, his best friend, sitting back and doing nothing."

"It would look like sense to me," Bonnie said tartly. "What does it matter what anybody thinks, anyway? You got all you could out of Bruce. Now, forget him, and stay out of it."

Saul turned slowly. "Out of what?"

"You know what I mean. There'll be hell raised around here over Frank Nearing. People will talk and sign petitions and make threats. Every time you go in a store the hot-stove wise guys will give you some inside dope on who killed Bruce." She smiled tolerantly. "I know you, Saul. You'll turn into the Voice of the People. Sooner or later you'll rub up against Millis, and if you get him mad enough he'll start wondering about you. And then it'll be too late."

Saul rinsed his hands and took down the towel. Bonnie's jibe had been just close enough to home to bring the color into his face. He said sarcastically, "What would I do without you, puss?"

"Swell up and bust," Bonnie said calmly.

"Tell me more," Saul said dryly.

"All right, I will. I'll tell you what to do. Whenever the funeral is, you show up at it. Tell the Duchess and her old man that it was a terrible thing, that they have your sympathy, then come back here and drink a cart of whisky and stay in bed for a week. When anybody asks you about it just say, 'We all have to die sometime,' and turn over and sleep. How's that?"

"Lousy," Saul said quietly, and went on, "Now I'll tell you what I'm *going* to do. The other night when Nearing jumped me and took me up to his room, he got way out of bounds. He was even out of bounds when he jumped Joe Mc-Kenzie and took that stuff. I'll not forget this." He smiled crookedly. "He's stuck his head out this time. I'll knock it off for him."

There was alarm in Bonnie's voice as she asked, "What are you going to do, Saul?"

"See him hang," Saul said briefly.

"Saul if you do, you're —"

"Quiet, puss," Saul said mildly. He went into his room across the hall and took off his shirt and Bonnie followed him, her dark eyes somber and angry. She sat on his bed and watched him put on a clean flannel shirt.

She said suddenly in a bitter voice, "I'll say it again, Saul. Let's get out of here. Now!"

"No."

"But Bruce is dead! You'll never find another sucker like him! We've got money, and we're in the clear! Why don't we go?"

"No."

Bonnie said scathingly, "Do you know what I've got a notion to do, Saul? I think I'll wait outside your room tonight and shoot through the window at you."

Saul turned slowly to look at her.

"Maybe you'd get what I'm trying to tell you, then!" Bonnie said bitterly. "Saul, I've been shot at! I'm scared! I want to get out of here!"

Saul laughed and turned to the mirror. "Nuts." He looped his tie over. "You weren't shot at. You're scared of your shadow. Besides that, I'm staying." He hesitated and said calmly, "You can go if you want, though."

Real panic mounted into Bonnie's eyes for a moment, but she sat motionless. The quick rise and fall of her breasts was the only sign of her agitation. Then she said baldly, "You want me out of here so you can make a pass at the Duchess, eh?"

Saul said wearily, "Yeah. Sure."

"What are you dressing up for?"

"My shirt was torn."

"Where are you going?"

Saul finished tying his tie, patted it, and then turned to face Bonnie. "Puss, I'm going to take a drink, maybe two, right here. Then I'll eat supper and come up here and put on my coat. You'll follow me and ask me where I'm going. Then I'll tell you I'm going over to pay my respects to Kelcy McIvor and her father. You'll

191

yell your head off, but that won't stop me. Understand, it won't stop me. And I'll probably hit you to shut you up." He smiled, without any humor. "Would you rather get hit now, or after supper? It doesn't matter to me when I do it."

McIvor's house lay right behind the store, facing the back street. It was a two-story affair of logs with a neat picket fence around it. When Saul entered the gate that night he could look through the window and see Mr. McIvor in conversation with a pair of townspeople. Nevertheless, Saul knocked on the door.

Kelcy answered it, and when she saw Saul her face lost a little of its gravity. She led him back through the hall into the kitchen, which was warm and dimly lighted from the lamp in a wall bracket by the big black stove.

Saul took the chair Kelcy offered, and waited until she sat down across the table from him.

"Is there any way I can help, Kelcy?" he asked.

Kelcy shook her head. "If you could only go in and help me talk to these people who are coming in," she said tonelessly. "Oh, they're kind and they mean well. But they hated him when he was alive. Now they pretend they didn't. None of them knew the lovable side of him — like we did."

Saul smiled sadly. "No. They were afraid of that wild streak. And it was what I liked in him, his spirit." Then he said, "But maybe you'd rather not talk about it, Kelcy."

"I don't mind — to you. But I won't talk about it to people who hint that it was murder and scandal."

Saul's face was grave. He said levelly, "Then you'd better not talk to me, Kelcy. Because I think it was murder."

"Saul!" Kelcy stared at him intently. "I see," she said softly. "That explains the bandage. You were in that mob?"

"Led it," Saul corrected. "I'm not ashamed of it, either, Kelcy. If I can stir up enough trouble to get Millis to use the information I have, I'll be content to take the blame."

"What information?"

"You tell me first about your finding Bruce, if you don't mind. Then I'll tell you what I know."

Kelcy told him all she knew, even about the conversation with Frank when they brought in Bruce's body. "If it was murder, would Frank Nearing have taken us to Horn Lake and helped search for Bruce? And if he was guilty, wouldn't he have told about Bruce's strychnine peddling? He didn't, Saul. At this very moment, Millis doesn't know where the strychnine came from."

Saul said in a voice edged with anger, "Why should he? If Nearing had betrayed that, wouldn't you have told Millis about that first day you met him? And he doesn't want that above everything."

"Why? Do you know anything about Frank Nearing?"

"Nothing. It's a hunch. Why would he have

193

blackmailed you, then, into keeping away from Millis?"

"I don't know," Kelcy faltered, and then her voice firmed. "But I don't think that was why he kept quiet. It was — well, a consideration for me, maybe."

Saul smiled wryly. "Kelcy, Kelcy, be careful. Walk with your eyes open."

"But I am, Saul! I don't think Frank Nearing is a killer."

"Wait." Saul folded his arms on the table top and said calmly, "For murder, you've got to have a motive, don't you?"

"Yes, and there is none. Why would Frank Nearing kill Bruce? Because he thought I'd told Bruce that I overheard something that first day in the hotel room? Nonsense! I didn't hear anything. That's too flimsy. Don't you see, if Frank Nearing killed Bruce over that he'd have to know what I overheard. And he'd have to kill me."

Saul smiled agreement. "All right, that's out. No motive there. But how do you like this? Bruce went up to Wailing River with a letter of Nearing's, a letter that came in the mail and that Bruce opened."

"Saul!"

"I'm telling the truth," Saul said earnestly. "Bonnie saw him steam the letter open over a teakettle on your storeroom stove."

Kelcy sat transfixed, and Saul went on gently, "Bonnie doesn't know what was in the letter. She refused to read it, and she tried to keep Bruce from opening it. But whatever was in that letter was so important, so secret, that Bruce thought he could go straight to Nearing and blackmail him with it. Bruce probably said something like this: 'Give me that strychnine you've got, and if you ever say a word about my bringing it in, about my peddling it, I'll tell Millis what I read in that letter.'" Saul leaned back in his chair. "Does that supply a motive? Nearing was afraid of what Bruce knew. He had to get him out of the way. He took him over to the height of land, left him poisoned food, and came back. If Bruce was discovered, nobody could prove Nearing poisoned him. He planted the bottle on Bruce to make it look like suicide. Nobody could supply a motive. And you're helping Nearing. Don't you see, Kelcy?"

Kelcy was silent for a full minute. "That's what Frank was trying to keep Bonnie from telling that day up in the hotel," she mused.

Saul said nothing, watching her. Kelcy shuddered suddenly and said, "It can't be, Saul. It just can't be!"

"It can! It is!"

"But he doesn't look like a killer!"

"They never do. Ask Millis. Look at the pictures of murderers."

Kelcy straightened her back and looked miserably at Saul. "Are you going to tell Millis?"

"It's not my brother," Saul said in a kindly voice. "It's up to you, Kelcy. I'm human enough to want to see Bruce's murderer punished. But

195

to see justice done, Bruce's name will have to be dragged through slime and muck. And I won't do that, Kelcy. I have no right to do it. It's up to you. Would you rather see a clever killer on the loose than tell Millis about Bruce stealing the letter? It's your choice."

Kelcy's face was gray, and she was trembling. Suddenly she put her face in her hands, and Saul came to his feet. But Kelcy wasn't crying. Saul watched impersonally while she suffered the agony of that choice, his eyes curious and probing and sly. Kelcy's hands came down on the table and she stared at the worn pattern of oilcloth for so long that Saul thought he was dismissed. He moved his feet, and the noise of it lifted Kelcy's glance to him.

"I'll do it, Saul," she said in a dull voice. "I guess I'm human enough to want to see Bruce's killer punished, too. Only, can't I wait? Can't I let him be buried in peace, without people knowing he was a common thief?"

Saul said gently, "Of course, Kelcy."

"And you'll come with me to Millis after the funeral?"

"Gladly." Saul hesitated. "I'd hold just one thing back from Millis, Kelcy. I wouldn't tell him about the strychnine, or where it came from. I wouldn't for two reasons. There's no use smearing Bruce any more than you have to. The opening of those letters will be all Millis wants. The other reason is Joe McKenzie. That poor devil has suffered agonies with that leg. Why punish him more?"

Kelcy said she wouldn't, and got unsteadily to her feet. And then the tears came in spite of her. It was the second time, and she couldn't help it. She buried her face in her hands, and then she felt Saul's hands on her shoulders as he drew her to him.

"Oh, Saul, it's so rotten — so damned, damned rotten!" She choked the words out against Saul's chest. "You're the only friend I have in the world, Saul — the only one!"

"Hush," Saul murmured. "Everybody loves you. Not as much as I do, maybe, but they do."

And Kelcy heard his declaration of love for her, and it didn't seem strange because she needed it so badly.

Chapter Fifteen

The day after the evening Saul had gone to see Kelcy, Bonnie knew she had lost him. Nothing was said, nothing was done, but she knew. They had fought a hundred times before, but the fights always had a pattern. There would be hot words, maybe blows, and sometimes for days afterward they would snarl at each other and think up cruel little ways to get even. But there always came a time eventually when Saul would swear and then laugh sheepishly, or Bonnie would come out of her sulk and kiss him, and the storm would be over.

This time, there was no storm.

Saul was polite and friendly to her, but she couldn't get into his mind. When she had cursed him that morning, he laughed at her. When she pleaded with him, he didn't answer her. He had the cool, contained, and satisfied manner of a man who has just settled a question in his mind, and who is experiencing the blessed relief of dearly purchased conviction. The Duchess, with her blonde good looks, her smile, her aloofness, had won the day — and the year. Soon, Bonnie knew, Saul would tell her about his new love, thinking it was news to her. And Bonnie would go.

The thing to do, Bonnie decided, was get away

from him. Move over to the other hotel and make him miss her. When he got tired of talking sweet nothings to that icicle and holding hands in the parlor, he would come back to her. But she knew he wouldn't, and yet she was going to put up the fight.

Saul was gone all morning. Bonnie moved her clothes over to the other hotel while he was absent. He came in to change his clothes at noon, and did not even remark on the emptiness of her room. He left, dressed in a black suit, and bade her a formal good day. He was going to the funeral that afternoon.

Bonnie remembered the night she had gone to the dance to watch Saul and Kelcy, unable to resist turning the knife in the wound. She was still unable to resist it, she thought bitterly, as she went up the stairs to change into a black dress and coat. There was nothing like watching your man make love to another woman at a funeral.

Bonnie didn't attend the services in the little frame church, but when the funeral procession filed out onto the newly shoveled path that led from the vestry to the graveyard next to the church, Bonnie slipped unobtrusively into the crowd. She saw Lute and Millis, dressed in sober black, with Frank Nearing. And Kelcy was between Saul and her father.

A light snow was falling from an overcast sky, and the new earth from the grave was powdered lightly. The edges of the hole were jagged, and crowbars had dug into the frozen earth, they had left polished black marks rimed with ground frost.

The services here were short, and Bonnie paid no attention to them. She was watching Saul and Kelcy. Mr. McIvor and Kelcy were dry-eyed through it all; Saul wore a suitably grave expression that made Bonnie's lip lift in a silent sneer. He had used that poor fool of a Bruce McIvor, lied to him and cheated him and framed him, and now he was pretending a well-mannered grief. Bonnie hated him at that moment as she had hated nothing before in her life.

After the services Saul and Kelcy stepped over to speak to Millis, and Bonnie turned away. She was almost out of the gate of the cemetery when she heard Saul calling: "Bonnie. Bonnie!"

She stepped off the path to wait for them, for Kelcy was on Saul's arm. She nodded to Nearing, Lute, and Millis as they passed her, feeling uncomfortable under the brief stare of Nearing's deep-set eyes.

Her handsome face was sullen and hostile when Saul and Kelcy stopped in front of her. Kelcy spoke, but Bonnie didn't.

"Can you come over to Millis' office with us, Bonnie?" Saul asked.

"What for?"

"Kelcy is going to tell Millis about Bruce and those letters he opened. They give Nearing a motive for Bruce's murder and she wants you to corroborate the story."

"Oh, so you told her that?" Bonnie asked.

"Of course," Saul said easily. But there was no easiness in his eyes, Bonnie saw. He had that alert, bland look of gall on his face that he wore whenever he faced a crisis of any sort. And that crisis Bonnie well understood. Suppose she were to blurt out now Saul's connection with Bruce and name him as the liar he was? That look on Saul's face was the warning, and Bonnie heeded it sullenly. Her hatred for Saul did not conquer either her good sense or her fear. One word about Saul's business and he would kill her, and Bonnie knew it. But there were other ways.

She smiled crookedly, looking at Kelcy, and said then roughly, "Both of you can go to hell. I don't know anything about any letters."

"I think you'll remember when Millis hauls you up before him this afternoon and makes you tell him," Saul pointed out.

"Well, he'll have to make me," Bonnie said curtly. "I'm not squealing on anyone for you — either of you."

She turned and walked on alone, her anger blazing now. So that was the way he'd bought himself into Kelcy's good graces, by squealing and trying to hang the murder on Nearing. Bonnie didn't care enough about Bruce to wonder if he had died by murder or suicide, or why. At the moment, she only saw this murder as an excuse for Saul to play the hero and the protector to Kelcy. She wished passionately that Millis would pry around until he discovered Saul's real business here. But Saul could be shrewd, and he was playing for high stakes.

She dropped in at the Star in the gone daylight, spoke to the cook, and then stepped across the street to the other hotel.

As she was going up the steps, someone else was coming down. She looked up and saw Lute, who silently touched his cap to her.

"Wait a minute," Bonnie called, when she was a step or so beyond him. Lute came up to the step she was on.

"If you want to keep Nearing out of more trouble, you better take a message to him, and right now."

"What's that?"

"Saul Chenard and Kelcy McIvor are on their way to Millis now to talk to him. They're going to tell him about the letters Bruce stole. They figure it'll give Nearing a motive for murdering Bruce."

"Well?"

"Tell Nearing to clam up," Bonnie said curtly. "They're going to send over for me to ask me about them, because I was with Bruce when he opened them, but I'll deny everything."

She couldn't see Lute's face in the near darkness, but she had the impression that he was staring at her with those pale observant eyes that never missed a trick.

"Millis will make you," Lute said slowly.

"Ha!" Bonnie laughed. "Let him try. I've faced cops before."

"He'll throw you in jail."

"So what? I eat, don't I?"

Lute thought a moment in silence, and Bonnie wondered what he was thinking.

"Listen," Lute said. "There's a shack, an empty shack, a couple of miles downriver from town. It's back off the river on the edge of a slough. It's a tight shack, and there's lots of wood there. Why don't you hide out there till this blows over? I'll take you down tonight with bedding and grub and everything you need."

"Why should I hide?" Bonnie demanded. "I tell you, Millis won't get anything out of me."

"You'll be sure he won't if he can't find you, won't you?"

Bonnie was about to refuse when the advantages of the scheme occurred to her. When Saul didn't have a witness to corroborate his story, he'd be wild. Would he miss her, and would he worry about her? And beyond that there was the solid pleasure she would get out of revenge. It was worth the inconvenience to see Saul squirm. And added to that was a kind of perverse desire to help Nearing, simply because she would be frustrating Saul.

"I might, at that," she said slowly, and then added, "But I'll have to put the cook wise over at the restaurant."

"Tell nobody!" Lute said curtly. "Just disappear. Will you?"

"Sure," Bonnie said lightly. "I like the idea. What's the shack like, just a heap?"

"No, trust me," Lute said, a faint excitement

in his voice. "I'll go tell Frank to deny everything. Then I'll drift around to a dozen stores and pick up your outfit. After dark I'll meet you on the river below the bend. You better go up and change clothes and start out right now, just so Millis won't break in at the last moment."

"O.K." Bonnie climbed a step, then paused and looked at Lute. "Say, Nearing didn't really poison Bruce, did he?"

"Hell, no!" Lute said. "I know what really happened. I'll tell you tonight."

Bonnie tripped up the stairs.

Lute hurried out into the cold dusk and went back to hitch up the dogs. That done, he drove down the main street and headed across the flats in front of the dozen or so people on the sidewalks. At the river he turned up it, vanished a mile or so above where the river twisted. He waited then out of sight the few minutes until full darkness, then turned the team around and retraced his route as far as the flats. There, however, he kept on the river trail, passed the town, and went downriver. It was dark now, and the lights of the town faded behind him, screened by the bush.

As he rounded the bend below, he kept an alert eye on the shore line, which was close and faintly visible.

Suddenly a voice called, "Hey!"

It was Bonnie. Lute whoaed the dogs and called, "All set. Come on and ride."

While he was talking, he reached down into the cariole, which contained only a bedroll, a tarp, a gun, and an ax. He brought out the ax in the darkness and leaned it against the tailboard.

Bonnie waded through the snow to the sled. Lute handed her into the cariole and she sat down, pulling the bedroll and tarp over her.

"Say," Bonnie said suddenly. "Either this is a big sled or you haven't much grub for me."

Lute's mittened hand settled around the ax handle. "You won't have to worry about that," he said gently, before he struck.

When the job was done, he straightened her out in the bottom of the cariole and covered her with the tarp. Then he turned the team and headed up the Raft. He was safe now, utterly safe. The two persons who had read his letter were dead, and would never talk. He would never know for sure if Bonnie had read the letter or not. If she had, Millis' probing would have brought her memory to bear on it, and Millis was one man who could make sense out of Carl's cryptic message. If she had not read it — well, a man never died because he was too careful.

Passing the town, Lute was remembering the sulphur spring on Swan Lake where the moose had gone through. A body's weight would break the ice and sink and the water would freeze over again, sealing death cleanly until distant spring. He mushed on up the river.

Chapter Sixteen

Saul still smarted when he thought of that session with Millis. It had started off well, with Millis interested but skeptical of the existence of any letters. He had sent for Bonnie, but the messenger couldn't find her. Then Saul and Millis had hunted for her. At last, Saul had reluctantly confessed that she might be hiding to spite him. Under Millis' hard questioning Saul had admitted that Bonnie was jealous of Kelcy. And before he realized it he had sketched enough of the story for Millis to get the whole picture of a tough, self-educated man trying to shake off an old love so that he might better himself with a new one. Millis had not commented, but behind his pale, skeptical eyes there was the Scot's puritan contempt for this libertine philosophy.

He had said sardonically, "Well, when you kiss and make up, bring her over to see me. And make it fast."

As Saul looked for Bonnie that night in all the likely places in Lobstick, he was remembering her prediction to him the day before. Bonnie had said that if he were left to himself, Saul would stir up Millis' curiosity to the point of danger. It wasn't dangerous yet, but Saul admitted to himself that he had confessed things he had never meant to.

His night's search was fruitless. So was the next day's. He alternated between a hot anger at Bonnie and concern over her. She had never done anything like this before, but then she had never had reason to be so jealous before. He combed his memory for a place she might be hiding. Lobstick wasn't big enough to hide in for long. The hotel told him that Bonnie had come in after the funeral and left immediately afterward, dressed for outdoors. Her trail blanked out there, just where it began. For a few dollars, of course, she might have bribed any one of the dozens of half-breed families in their mean shacks on the fringe of town to hide and feed her. Nothing short of a search warrant could find her in any of these shacks.

That evening Saul admitted defeat. After a lonely supper he set out for Millis' office, and as he walked the hard-packed road in the cold he cast about for phrases that would make his predicament less ridiculous to Millis.

The office was dark, but at Saul's knock Millis came through from the house, lighted the lamp, let him in, and threw some coal in the big iron stove in the corner.

Sitting in the chair opposite the desk, Saul told Millis that he couldn't find Bonnie. Millis tilted back in his chair, unbuttoned his brown tunic, and let Saul flounder through his explanations. His blue eyes reflected no sympathy at all; there was neither amusement nor censure in his broad high-colored face.

207

When Saul was finished, Millis said roughly, "You've lived with her for a couple of years now. You ought to know her friends. Have you asked them?"

"She hasn't got many. Yes, I've asked them."

"And you think she's holed up in some breed's shack just to make you worry over her?"

"I do."

Millis sighed gustily and shook his head. "When I joined up with the police," he mused sourly, "I had a notion I'd be hunting dangerous characters on a pretty sorrel gelding. And look what I've got. I'm a referee in Indian adultery. I'm a nursemaid to every bloody family row. I bring the law to the female back-fence riots. And now, by God, I'm hunting a lost love for you."

"Not for me," Saul said testily. "I only want her to confirm my story."

"Why did you ever bring it to me in the first place?"

"Because I think Nearing killed Bruce McIvor."

"And what's it to you, personally, if he did?" Millis demanded. "Don't bother to mention justice. You didn't give a damn about young McIvor. Nobody with sense did, outside his family, and you've got sense. Why do you bother?"

"You mean you want me to hold back information I can give you that might lead to the discovery of a murderer?"

"You know damn well I don't mean that," Millis answered. "What I'm trying to point out, and having a hell of a hard time getting across to you, is that I think you've waited for a peculiar time to tell me about those letters. Do you get me?"

"No."

"Those letters were stolen weeks ago. Day before yesterday you told me about it. Why? Do you want me to tell you why?"

Saul didn't answer.

"It's because you're making a large and clumsy play for Kelcy McIvor," Millis said sourly. "That's your affair, normally. I have no objection to any man making a hero of himself in front of a girl. But what I do object to, specifically, is your withholding that information about the letters for three weeks or a month until you saw a chance to use it for your own good. Or" — his voice took on a savage irony now — "did it just occur to you that legally young McIvor was a mail robber?"

"He was my friend," Saul murmured.

Millis' jaw clamped shut, and a look of ineffable disgust was on his face. "Lovely," he snarled, "just lovely! What touching loyalty! Phooey! Nuts!" He slapped a thick hand on the desk. "My friend, I'll have a nice present for you when I get more pressing business cleared away. It will be in the shape of a very stiff fine and a court reprimand for withholding information. And if there was a jail here instead of this single cell where I'd have to feed you and put up with you twelve hours a day, you'd be behind bars. Now get the hell out of here and let my head ache in peace!"

Saul went out quietly, and Millis slowly regained a measure of composure. He was a fool to give way to his temper like that, he supposed, but a man, even a policeman, can bear only so much. He rubbed his eyes with his hand and tilted back in his chair, his face morose and somber. He could visualize the report he would send out this next week. No progress on the Mary Paulin case; a new death under suspicious circumstances; robbery of the mails (which would result in McIvor's losing the post mastership, he supposed); a riot; and, lastly, no arrests. The inspector would read the report, decide that Millis was in over his head, and send help. He'd be glad for the help if it weren't an admission of his inability to hold down his job. His request last week that no help be sent and his assurance that the case would break soon had been an empty gesture of stiff-necked pride. He'd been a fool to ask it, the inspector a fool to grant it. He wondered gloomily who they'd send up here in his place when it was all settled, and what piddling, humiliating job he'd be shifted to.

And again, as he had done a thousand times in these last two days, he tried to understand this. Was Mary Paulin's murder tied up in any way with Bruce McIvor's? Nothing pointed to it, but Millis' hunch, with not one iota of proof to back it up, was that it did tie up. And what was Nearing's part in this? Against his better judgment he liked Nearing, so he had to fight prejudice to begin with. He rejected the idea that Nearing would poison McIvor. He also rejected the idea that McIvor committed suicide. And yet he couldn't reject both. This new evidence that Saul Chenard and Kelcy had presented him with was important. He had been waiting for Bonnie Tucker's evidence to confirm it, but now Bonnie Tucker was hiding. He could bluff it through with Nearing, he was certain, because he remembered that obscure talk between Bonnie and Nearing that afternoon in Saul's hotel. They were talking about the letters, only he hadn't known it then.

His case against Nearing simply resolved into this: Nearing could have poisoned the food (although autopsy showed only poisoned tea in Bruce's stomach), and left Bruce with the food on the height of land to die. The trouble with that was that Nearing had willingly helped to find the body. He also had no motive for the murder — unless it was contained in those letters Bruce stole. And behind it all loomed the fact that Nearing refused to state why he had taken Bruce to the height of land, and had refused to state where the strychnine came from. He was confronted with a man who helped to uncover evidence against himself, and refused to give evidence that would help him.

Millis raised his head then and listened to Charlie's soft tread on the stairs. The Indian was leaving. That Indian was a curious customer, too, close-mouthed and loyal and secretive. For that matter, so was Westock, the other partner, although there was nothing much to him. Quiet and dumb, maybe smart professionally, but a nonentity otherwise.

Charlie passed through the office, bade Millis a soft good night, and went out. Millis heaved himself out of his chair and blew out the light, knowing the time had come for his talk with Nearing.

He tramped up the stairs, knocked, and stuck his head in the door. Nearing was peeling off his shirt.

"Come in," Frank invited.

Millis yawned and came in. He looked around the room and said conversationally, "I got the kid's school report last mail. She's brighter than me." He smiled ruefully and settled into a chair. "It's a good thing she is, too, but it's not saying much for her."

"You're too modest," Frank said. "Too suspicious, too, but you're a cop. When do I get out of the doghouse?"

"So you think this room is a doghouse?" Millis jibed.

Frank grinned. "You know what I mean." He tossed his tobacco pouch to Millis and settled back on the bed. "I've read myself blind. It's no fun getting out at night. I'll look like a toadstool in a few more days. You still think they'd mob me?"

Millis clumsily concentrated on his smoke and

did not look up. "No. The talk's still there, but it's off boil now. I think it's safe — only I don't want you to go."

"But why not?" Frank demanded. "Hell, if you're going to arrest me, do it. If you're not, let me go."

Millis lighted his cigarette and returned the pouch. "Back to Christmas Valley?"

"Yes. After the next mail, I'll hit for the shack."

Millis grunted. "You watch that mail plane pretty close, don't you?"

"Who doesn't — especially if they come from outside?"

"Ever miss any mail you've been expecting?" Millis asked idly, looking up at Frank.

Frank knew instantly what he meant. He said, "No. Why should I?"

"I just wondered if young McIvor had stolen anything before he hooked those two letters of yours and opened them." Millis' pale eyes were watching him.

"So you know about them," Frank said softly.

"Of course. I'm a cop, a paid snoop. I know a lot of things I don't talk about."

"For instance."

"Well, I know you had a motive for taking Bruce over to the height of land, now. It was something in those letters."

"But what?"

Millis smiled. "Give me time. I'll find that out, too." He hesitated and then said gently, "Funny, but every new thing I learn about you just makes it tougher for you. Why don't you come clean with it and get it over with?"

"With what?"

"What was in those letters. What —"

"Letter," Frank corrected. "He opened one of Lute's, too. That was the second."

"So I heard. But what was in yours that would make you take McIvor up there and leave him — maybe poison him too? If you're a criminal, I'll know it next mail, because we're looking you up. If you aren't a criminal, why hold out on me?"

Frank was silent a long time, scowling at the pouch on the bed. Absently he picked it up and rolled and lighted a smoke. Afterward he held the burning match in his hand, staring at the flame until it burned his fingers. He dropped it, stepped on it; then, remembering this was not his room, he picked the match up and held it in his hand.

"Millis, can you imagine a man refusing to explain his actions simply because if he does explain them he'll lose something he wants pretty badly?"

Millis scowled. "Yes," he said slowly. "But like what?"

"That's it. If I tell you, I'm apt to lose it. But if you'll wait until the mail plane Friday brings a letter I'm expecting, I'll tell you. Friday I can talk."

Millis stared at him searchingly. "Mystery and stuff, eh?"

"It's so simple you'll laugh," Frank said. "Friday I'll tell you every blessed thing about me you want to know — why I took Bruce over there, and —"

"About where the strychnine came from?"

Frank shook his head. "I can't."

"Can't or won't?"

Frank said nothing.

Millis said obliquely, "My God, the girl's trying to hang you. Why don't you tell where the poison came from?"

Frank said woodenly, "What are you talking about?"

Millis grinned. "I don't know. I'm just guessing. You don't look like a man who'd use strychnine. Bruce McIvor was the kind. I just figured you were keeping still about it because Kelcy didn't want it known."

Frank said, "What did you mean about the girl trying to hang me?"

"Just that. She told me about the letter of yours Bruce stole."

"She did?"

"She figures something in that letter Bruce read made it necessary for you to shut his mouth."

Frank didn't speak for a moment as he studied the end of his cigarette. "Nothing will ever make it necessary for me to kill a man," he said slowly. "I'll tell you now, I'll tell her."

"Sure, sure," Millis said. He rose. "This about Friday's mail is straight, is it? It'll help me settle this?"

"I doubt it," Frank said. "It's just my part

215

in it — all of my part. But I'm telling you now, Millis, and you'll come to believe it, that Bruce had to commit suicide or die by accident. I didn't do it."

"Maybe," Millis said, and bade him good night.

Chapter Seventeen

An hour after breakfast, Corporal Millis knew he was up against a stone wall in this McIvor business. Last night's disclosures by Frank had hamstrung him, rendered him impotent, although he hadn't realized it at the time. Maybe he'd been sleepy last night and missed it. This morning, it appeared to him with appalling clarity. Nearing would tell him on Friday why he took young McIvor to the height of land, thereby disclosing what was in the letter. And obviously there would be nothing there to give Nearing a motive, or else Nearing wouldn't tell him about it. Everything would be explained, reasonably and without lurid disclosures. Which would leave Millis where Nearing was now — convinced that Bruce had died by suicide or accident. If he wasn't convinced, then he must go off on an entirely new tack.

Millis was at his desk, and he groaned. He didn't know why he hated so to acknowledge that Bruce McIvor committed suicide, but he did. He swore bitterly and looked bleakly upon the coming day. He was sick of this business, sick as hell of it, and he was plagued by it. But since he was helpless till Friday, he might as well forget it. There was other work to do, namely, hammer away at this Mary Paulin business — which was even worse.

He came to his feet, slammed his chair back against the wall, and got his coat and cap. He was almost to the door when he remembered he hadn't locked his desk.

Coming back, he opened the bottom drawer to make sure the bottle of scorched strychnine was in there. Exhibit A, he thought, in a trial that was not going to come off. Still, he must go through the motions and send it out for routine analysis and report. Hell, what did they expect was in the bottle if it wasn't strychnine? He locked the desk and went out.

His first call was at the Star Café. Of the waitress he asked, "Miss Tucker back yet?"

"Not yet, sir," the girl said.

"Chenard in?"

"Upstairs in his room."

Millis went up, knocked on Saul's door, and entered. Saul's face was haggard as he looked up from lacing his boots.

"Did Bonnie come to you?" Saul asked quickly.

"No. So she hasn't come back, eh?"

Saul's face fell. "No. I'm going out again this morning. I'm going to look in every room of every breed's shack, and if they complain to you I don't give a damn."

Millis nodded, and observed shrewdly, "Miss her, do you?"

Saul stood up and looked levelly at Millis. "Damn right I do," he said. "I'm not ashamed of it, either."

"Why should you be?"

"I shouldn't. I was just remembering those cracks you made last night. Besides that, I'm worried about her."

"You think she's taken poison over you? I doubt it," Millis said dryly.

"All right, laugh. But I've known her a long time, and this isn't funny."

"Right," Millis said. He started for the door. "Next time you try to handle two women at once, remember that. It isn't funny."

Down on the street, Millis hesitated. Bonnie Tucker was the person he wanted to talk to, and she was gone. He thought about that for a moment, and smiled at the memory of Saul Chenard's face. He didn't envy these Lotharios; they paid for what they got, and in a coin that wasn't worth it. He considered requizzing the dozen of Mary Paulin's admirers and then remembered that most of them were working out in the bush, hauling wood or trapping. He'd have to save them till tonight, when they were in.

And that left him with nothing to do, on either this case or McIvor's. There was nothing left but to go back to the office and write on his report, those bald facts that no amount of polishing and restating could cushion.

Back in his office and seated at the desk, he unlocked his desk drawers and brought out some forms. Lying there on some papers was the bottle of strychnine, its cork scorched, the powder inside a little browned.

He picked it up and held it in his palm, regarding it curiously. He might as well get that ready to go out, too. He remembered reading somewhere about strychnine death. It was agonizing, and a man was conscious all through it. The convulsions bent a man backward almost double, and every muscle constricted until it almost burst. A man strangled to death, really. Under the frenzied clamp of those muscles his respiration was paralyzed. He lay there with every muscle rock-hard to bursting, his heart racing, his back arched, black terror in his mind, and died for lack of air. Bruce McIvor had died a hell of a death, the death he had supplied to a lot of animals. It was a wry justice, Millis thought as he regarded the bottle idly. He held up the bottle to the light and shook it. It was as fine as face powder or flour, and clung to the side of the bottle in a gray film. Yes, it looked like his wife's face powder.

He tried to recall what the strychnine seized in that death at Shore Lake looked like, and he thought it was coarser grained. But not much.

Aware that he shouldn't be tampering with evidence, he jabbed his paper knife in the cork and extracted it. Somewhere he'd heard a trapper tell about baiting a set on the spot in a high wind. Some of the powder had blown out of the hole in a slice of moose liver and the man had breathed it. It speeded up his heart until he was dizzy, and then the effects died off. The stuff was dynamite, and yet it looked as innocent as frost scrapings.

Unconsiously holding his breath, Millis poured a little of the stuff onto a sheet of clean paper and examined it gingerly. Yes, it looked like face powder or scorched flour, for it was brownish. He had begun to breath again, not noticing he had, until he was suddenly aware of a faint odor. He sniffed it cautiously. That had the smell of burned bread.

Something began ticking in the back of Millis' mind. He held his breath and leaned close to the brownish powder. Certain there was none of it in the air, he sniffed cautiously. There was the distinct smell of flour there, the same smell as around the stove when his wife began to make flour gravy.

He leaned back slowly and looked at the powder. If — just if — that stuff was flour, where would it leave him? Bruce McIvor couldn't commit suicide with flour. Then the strychnine must have been in his food! But his stomach was empty, except for the tea. Could strychnine cling to dry tea? No. Then sugar? Ah, that was it. Of course that was it! The sugar had fallen in the fire and burned, leaving no evidence. But if Bruce made his tea, dumped sugar in it, and drank off a cup to warm him, then his death would be explained.

And then Millis' Scots common sense hauled him up. Wait a minute, my friend. That's too easy. You're supposing this is flour. What if it's strychnine? You don't know what scorched strychnine looks like, smells like, or tastes like. All you know is that it kills you. Keep your mind open and put this stuff away and send it out for analysis.

But the implications of that scorched powder there before him were stunning. He had a nearly irresistible impulse to wet his finger, dip it in the powder, and taste it. He didn't.

And then the answer crashed down in his mind. Doc Hardy could make an analysis!

Millis came to his feet, wildly excited and cursing. He'd been a fool! Why hadn't he thought of Doc immediately? The reason was, of course, that he hadn't doubted it was strychnine before. The coroner's verdict was death from strychnine. He was sending it through the regular channels with his report for a routine analysis. Now, he had to find out! He knew one moment of doubt. Was the analysis a laboratory matter?

That vanished as he shakily poured the powder back into the bottle, corked it, and pocketed it. Yanking his coat and cap off the hook, he slammed out the door.

Once outside, he remembered his dignity, but in spite of it he was out of breath when he arrived at Doc Hardy's office. The nurse was in the surgery, which gave onto the hospital, and she was reading a book at the doctor's desk.

Millis barely greeted her. "Where's Doc?"

"Gone for the day. A man up at Gordon's Mill got a log dropped on his leg and crushed," the girl said ungrammatically.

Millis calmed down somewhat, but he was only temporarily at a loss. "Where's Doc's books?"

The girl pointed to the wall behind him, where old-fashioned glass-door bookcases contained row on row of medical books.

Millis looked at them and the despair of ignorance seized him. "Listen," he said. "Do you know anything about poisons?"

"Antidotes?"

"No, analysis. Can you find them in these books?"

The girl smiled and shook her head. "I'm afraid I can't, Corporal Millis. I'll look through them, though."

"For a week, I'll bet, and still not find anything," Millis growled.

He cast his glance again over the books. On the bottom shelf was a one-volume encyclopedia, the only title that made sense to him.

He had an idea. Kneeling, he pulled out the encyclopedia and pessimistically leafed through it until he came to "Strychnine." There were only a few lines about it, and he read them halfheartedly. But at the end, his attention stiffened. Strychnine, it said, was soluble in alcohol, ether, or chloroform.

Millis put it away and said, "Has Doc got ether here?"

"Why, yes, of course. Why?"

"Are you sure it's ether?"

The girl smiled uneasily. "It's something you can't mistake. If it isn't ether, then I've been giving the patients something else."

"Put me up some in a bottle."

Millis took the bottle she gave him, thanked the bewildered girl, and hurried home again. He locked the doors of his office, house and outside, and then settled back in his chair.

He took out the strychnine bottle and uncorked it, then uncorked the ether bottle. He must remember, just in case he was on the wrong track, to save some of the powder.

He poured half the contents of the bottle into the ether.

It clotted gummily on the surface, then settled. He shook the ether bottle and let it settle again.

The powder was not dissolving! He watched it for two minutes, during which it was still visible.

Settling back in his chair, he uncorked the bottle of strychnine, poured some out in his palm, and tasted it.

It was flour.

Millis sat immobile, his excitement under control. His brain was working logically now, without haste, with all the cunning of which it was capable.

Nearing killed Bruce McIvor. Any other statement didn't make sense. McIvor couldn't have committed suicide with flour; therefore, the grub left him contained the poison. Frank Nearing had promised to tell what was in his letter on Friday. Perversely, Millis still believed that. In his belief (or ignorance) that the strychnine would never be analyzed, Frank would supply the only thing missing — a motive. If he told the truth, then the case would be sewn up tighter than a shroud — motive, given voluntarily; method, already known; and proof, which Millis had in his hands.

If Frank wasn't alarmed, if Millis played dumb, there wouldn't be a hitch. There was the risk that if Millis didn't jail him, Frank might escape. To where, though, in these thousands of miles of bush? On the other hand, if Millis arrested him Frank would clam up and they might never explain the murder.

Millis thought of this for a full hour, weighing risk against risk. At the end of that hour, he silently put away the ether and the flour and locked the drawer. He'd already decided what he was going to do.

He was going to keep his mouth shut, giving Frank his freedom, until Friday.

Chapter Eighteen

Friday was a year arriving for at least two persons in the Millis household. A storm broke on Thursday, a howling, hammering fury that by noon had piled drifts head-high against the store windows on the south side of Lobstick's street. Frank and Millis watched it with a deepening gloom. There was a pattern to these storms: three days of snow, and then it turned off diamond clear. The plane couldn't come in on Friday through this.

But Friday dawned bright and cloudless, with a smothering, nose-pinching cold. As Millis dressed that morning he looked out over the town and saw the smoke from the breakfast fires rising straight and white and high. He put on his dress tunic of scarlet that morning, for obscure reasons of ceremony. If things went right, this would be a big day in his life. His good morning at breakfast was a cheery one as he observed Frank already at the table. He'd gambled that Frank wouldn't make a break for it, and it seemed that he'd won.

Afterward there were chores to do and mail to get off, and the morning passed with blessed swiftness. The noonday meal on Friday was always early on account of the plane, and Millis ate it alone. He was in the office putting on his coat when Frank came in. He was dressed for outdoors.

"Where are you going?" Millis asked.

"To meet the plane."

"I'll get your mail," Millis said. "I'll get it quicker than you could."

"Swell, but I'd like to see the plane off. Lute's leaving."

Millis stared at him. "Westock?"

"That's right. He has to go outside."

Millis thought quickly, a frown on his face. He shook his head and said, "Sorry, Frank, but you better stay here. The whole town's out on mail day, and I don't want another scrap on my hands."

"But damn it, Lute's leaving!"

"Sorry." Millis smiled to take the curse off his edict. "After today, things will be different. You've stood it for days, you can stand it another hour. I'll tell Westock good-by for you."

Frank glared at him in impotent anger. Behind the easygoing affability of Millis there was an iron will. He got his way and made you like it. He could take you into protective custody and make you more of a prisoner than a penitentiary could. Frank fought down his anger with an effort. A few more hours of this and he could hit out for the Wailing — if today's mail brought confirmation of his claim from the recorder's office at Fort Resource. And as Millis said, he could get Frank's letter much quicker than he could

227

himself. Lute would have to leave without a send-off, but that wasn't serious. There was nothing they had to say to each other except good-by. Frank had wanted to thank him for keeping so closemouthed, and that was all.

He sank into a chair and said resignedly, "All right, Millis. Only hurry it up."

Millis hurried out into the bright cold. So Westock, his chief witness, was leaving, was he? Millis thought about that while he walked over to the main street and down it, and by the time he was abreast of McIvor's store he'd made up his mind.

The flats by the river were smooth and spotless with the new snow except where the faithful plane greeters had broken a trail to the riverbank.

On fair days the plane sometimes ran ahead of schedule, and today the kids and loafers had anticipated this. There were a dozen or so of them on the bank, stamping their feet and hunching their shoulders in the bitter cold.

Millis picked out Lute Westock easily. He stood a little to one side of the main group, not a part of it, his fat duffel bag beside him in the snow. He was dressed in boots and sheepskin coat.

When Millis came up to him and greeted him, Lute answered quietly. Millis stood beside him, stamping his feet, and accidentally stepped on the duffel bag. He glanced down at it, observed it with apparent surprise, and looked up at Lute.

"What's the luggage?"

"I'm going out," Lute answered. "Didn't Frank tell you?"

"Outside? You mean you're leaving on the plane?"

"That's right." Lute's pale opaque eyes regarded Millis carefully. And then Millis put on his act. He seemed embarrassed and troubled by turns, and then he spoke quietly, apologetically.

"I wish you wouldn't."

"Why not?"

"We-l-l, I'm going to need you."

Lute smiled and shook his head. "I can't imagine what for, Corporal Millis, but I'm afraid I have to."

"How's that?"

Lute said gravely, "Frank and I have got a backer for a proposition that Frank thinks is pretty good. He's flown up from the States for two days, and I'm to meet him outside."

"Can't he wait?"

"He could, but he won't. He's a big promoter and he hasn't got much time for small fry. But if he'll listen to us, I think we can sell him on it."

Millis shook his head and said, "If I were you I'd go back to the hotel and put your proposition in writing. I'll hold the plane so your letter will get out on it."

Lute frowned. "I don't understand."

"You better not go out, that's all," Millis said mildly. "I need you here."

"But you don't understand," Lute said earnestly. "This is our chance, the one Frank's been working on for over a year. If we miss it, we're sunk."

"That's tough. I'll radio our man and explain, and maybe he'll make a date for later."

Lute seemed baffled, and in his eyes was a look of grave concern. "But you can't do that," he protested. "You can't ruin the fortunes of two people on a whim."

"It's not a whim," Millis said stubbornly. "I told you I need you here."

"But what for?"

Millis was silent a moment, debating whether or not to tell him. His caution prompted him not to. "You'll know in an hour or so when you drop around to my office."

"It's about Frank, isn't it? Can't you ask me now whatever you want me to answer?"

Millis knew that was impossible. You didn't quiz your most important witness in a murder case before the arrest was made, then turn him loose to disappear.

"I'm afraid not," he said gently. "Understand, I wouldn't do this if it wasn't important, more important than your business. If you've got a good thing there, somebody else will finance it. I'll even use what influence I have to help you. But you can't go out on this plane, Westock."

Lute's gaze locked with his, and for a moment they stared stubbornly at each other. The distant drone of the plane was faintly audible, but neither of them looked up for it.

"I don't believe you can stop me," Lute said grimly.

Millis smiled unpleasantly. "I'd hate to have you call me on that," he murmured.

Lute saw the mistake he had made. He said earnestly, a touch of desperation in his voice, "But can't you see my side, Millis? I've knocked around at any job for months, living like a dog and sending Frank all the money I could spare! We've sweated and slaved and poured our guts into this, and now it'll go out the window if I don't see this man! Can't you radio ahead and have a policeman follow me? Do anything you want, only let me see this man."

Millis felt like a cur. He was a fair man, and there was nothing fair about this. On the other hand, there was nothing fair about murder. And if he let Westock go, to disappear when he heard of Frank's arrest, he'd be officially labeled an idiot, which he wasn't. No, he had to hold him. And, because he wouldn't have been human if he wasn't angry at being put in a false light, Millis spoke a little roughly, with exasperation.

"Hell, I don't like this any more than you do, Westock. I'd help you if I could. This afternoon, when it's been explained to you, you'll see why I had to do it. No, you can't go out on this plane. That's final."

For a moment Millis saw a wild glint in Lute's pale eyes, a brash temper that he had never suspected in the man.

"Nothing I can do, nothing I can say, no bond

231

I can post, will change your mind?" Lute asked slowly.

The plane was near now, the time pressing. Millis said, "No, nothing will make me," and turned and started for the other group.

He paused then, and looked back at Westock, who was standing alone, a tall solid man with the most baleful eyes Millis had ever seen. Millis called, "Come over to the office at two, Westock. You'll see why I did this."

Lute didn't answer. He picked up his duffel and tramped back up the trail toward town.

Millis watched the plane land on the river, sending curtains of the new loose snow scudding in plumes behind it as it taxied over to the bank. He exchanged a few words with the pilot as the mail was unloaded, then, after the plane had left, followed the team up to McIvor's store.

The mail was taken into the post office, where Kelcy was waiting to sort it. She looked pale to Millis, as he watched her direct the placing of the sacks. When they were alone, the wicket boarded up, Kelcy said, "Are you guarding the mail now, Corporal Millis?"

"Meaning I don't trust you, Kelcy? You know better." Millis was quiet a moment, watching her. "What's the matter with you? You look like hell."

Kelcy smiled faintly. "I feel like hell, if you want to know the truth. I — guess I haven't bounced back yet."

"You never will if you stay sour."

"Why shouldn't I?" Kelcy asked bitterly. "It's

a rotten world, with rotten people in it."

"Like Nearing?"

"Yes, like Frank Nearing."

Millis stirred faintly and sighed. "You're young. You can take a kick like that. When you're as old as I am, it hits harder."

Kelcy looked at him curiously. "So you're beginning to believe now that Nearing did it? I mean, really believe it? You've suspected it all along."

Millis said quietly, "I don't just suspect it any more, I know it."

He was not prepared for what he saw in Kelcy's face. It was something like pain that hovered behind her eyes, and was fought down in a few seconds. He might as well break the news to her now, because she'd see the proof soon.

He told her he wanted all of Nearing's mail, and that he'd help her sort it. They worked an hour, Kelcy's swiftness making up for Millis' deliberate movements. When they were finished, there was one letter for Frank Nearing. It bore the postmark of Fort Resource and the printed legend of the recorder's office.

"When will you get through with this?" Millis asked.

"Two hours, perhaps. Why?"

"Come over to the office afterward, will you?"

Kelcy asked, "Is it something about that letter?"

Millis nodded and went out. Here was what he'd been waiting for, the last loose end in a tangled case.

He let himself into the office and looked around him. Nearing wasn't there. Millis stifled his impatience, peeled off his coat, and then stepped over to the tiny cell of four-by-fours. He unlocked the padlock and opened the cell door.

Frank was coming down the stairs as Millis started up them. There was a deep excitement in Frank's face as Millis handed him the letter in silence. Frank hurried back up the stairs, entered his room, went over to the window, and clumsily ripped the envelope open.

He read the letter, his face strained and tense, and suddenly he smiled. Millis watched him without comment as Frank finished and turned to him.

"I guess fairy stories come true after all," Frank murmured. "Read it."

Millis read it. The letter merely said the claim was recorded, repeated the figures Frank had given, and assigned a number to it.

Millis felt there was something here that he didn't understand, and asked in a normal voice, "What's the story?"

"That's Christiansen's old claim on Christmas Creek," Frank said. "There was ore there and he didn't find it. I did. But I found it before enough time had elapsed to make the claim forfeit. That letter Bruce opened was from the recorder's office, giving the rules of claim forfeiture. Bruce put two and two together, got up to the shack while I was away, had enough of a look to confirm his suspicions, then tried to blackmail me for a share in the mine.

"He had me over a barrel. I had three weeks to go before the old claim was forfeit, and in those three weeks anybody could have come in up there and fought me over the claim. If Bruce talked, I was sunk. I didn't trust him to keep quiet, because I'd seen him drunk and heard you say he was a rummy. Rather than take a chance on his blabbing it some night when he was tight, I had to get him away from people and planes and radios — away from everything, where he couldn't hurt me. I remembered Weymarn over on Horn Lake. I knew Weymarn would feed him, but wouldn't spare him dogs to get back to Lobstick and wouldn't bring him back. Bruce would be over there where his talk wouldn't harm me." He grinned. "That's why I didn't want you searching Christmas Valley for him, like Kelcy suggested. You'd have turned up my strike, and the news would have been out. That's why I took you over to Horn Lake, away from the strike. That one damned secret, Millis, is what I've been trying to keep. What do —" He paused.

Millis was staring at him, transfixed, his jaw sagging a little in amazement.

Frank laughed at the sight of him. "I told you it would be so simple you wouldn't believe it."

Millis said something then. It was spoken with deep pity, with a bare belief, and it was something that Millis dragged out of childhood and the memory of a Scots grandfather who would have said the same thing.

235

"Man," he said gently, "are ye daft?"

"I wouldn't know," Frank said easily. "I don't think so."

Millis' mouth closed with a little click of his teeth. He said courteously, "I have something for you downstairs, Frank. Go ahead."

Going down the stairs, Millis unfastened the flap of his holster.

Frank walked up to the desk and turned to face Millis, who said gently, "See that cell with the door open, Nearing? Get inside."

"But —"

"Get in there, I said!" Millis' voice was cold and savage and angry. His gun was in his hand now, low at his side, pointed at Frank, some six feet away.

Something in Millis' tone, a wildness and an anger and a hatred, warned Frank that this was no time to argue.

He walked in the cell and watched Millis close and lock the door on him.

"Why?" Frank asked.

Millis went over to the desk, unlocked it, and returned with the bottle.

"Is that the bottle we found under Bruce McIvor?" Millis asked.

Frank took it through the bars, examined it, and handed it back. "That's it. Some of the stuff is gone."

"That's right. It was tested. That white stuff that was in there was flour."

Frank just stared at him, bewildered. "Flour?"

"Flour, not strychnine! That means Bruce McIvor didn't commit suicide. He didn't have any strychnine to do it with. So there's only one thing left, Nearing. The food you left him was poisoned. It was the sugar." Millis raised a stubby hand, spread his fingers, and started ticking them off, his voice implacable. "One, you struck an ore body, and whether you got it depended on its being kept a secret. Two, Bruce discovered that secret. Three, you put strychnine in the grub you gave him and took him up to the height of land and left him. Four, Bruce was found dead from strychnine poisoning."

Millis' hands sank to his side. If he heard the knock on his office door, he pretended he hadn't. "Motive, method, and corpse. Figure it out. Altogether, it spells hanging, Nearing."

Chapter Nineteen

Frank sank down on the cot. His mind simply refused to work. He heard Millis speak and then saw McIvor. He heard her say, "I let Dad sort the mail, because I wondered —" She paused. "Is that Frank Nearing?"

Frank didn't hear any more. He was vaguely aware of Millis talking, of Kelcy talking. Slowly, lumberingly, the significance of what Millis had said was sinking into his mind and flagging it into thought. Not the part about hanging, for that didn't register. It was the part about the strychnine — or flour. He considered that a moment, slowly and thoughtfully and critically. Bruce couldn't have committed suicide with flour, true. (He wouldn't have carried flour in that sort of bottle, and besides, Frank remembered that bottle.) Then his food must have been poisoned, his sugar, of course, because that would take the strychnine. True. And only three persons had the chance to put the strychnine in the sugar — himself, Charlie, and Lute.

He heard the door open again, and heard Charlie's voice. He knew that would be Charlie coming in without the letter he'd been waiting for in McIvor's store to tell him the bad news. He heard Millis and Charlie talking, heard the

238

conversation grow sharp and three-cornered.

He was thinking about the three of them there at the shack, and immediately he thought of Lute. He recognized that as prejudice, and thought of Charlie as the poisoner. Nonsense. He himself didn't do it. So he settled on Lute. Why would Lute poison Bruce? He wouldn't; he didn't know him, didn't associate with him, stood to lose nothing if Bruce talked about the mine.

Millis' and Charlie's voices were raised in anger, and Frank barely noted it. He must leave Lute's motive for the present and think of the means. The grub was packed the night before they left, the strychnine bottle set on the bookshelf. Of course! Lute knew it was strychnine and he sat up guarding Bruce all night! He could have poisoned the sugar, and filled the strychnine bottle with flour. He was beginning to feel a gathering excitement now, and his mind was working better, faster.

Bruce stole the strychnine. Why? He didn't know. To take the evidence against him, to poison his captors, to poison their dogs so they couldn't go on to the height of land? Frank's mind clamped on that last possibility, and then it came to him. That day they left Bruce on the height of land when he went back to get tobacco! He went back to poison the dogs! That explained his strange bet with Frank on how long it would take them to get to Lobstick.

Millis was shouting, Charlie's soft voice was raised in wrath, and still Frank didn't hear. Lute could have done it, did do it, but why? His mind beat about that question for seconds, and then Frank pulled it up and directed it. Lute was hiding because his wife was persecuting him. Did Bruce know that? No, he couldn't — yes, he could! That letter of Lute's Bruce had opened! But Lute wouldn't kill Bruce to keep him from telling of his hiding out to dodge alimony payments. What had Bruce said that night to Lute? "When I get back to a newspaper, I can find out why you're hiding out." Alimony cases weren't in newspapers. Then it was something else in the letter, not the alimony business, or why the mention of a newspaper? Immediately, Frank's memory slipped to the letter from Carl that Lute had shown him. Was that a forgery (it could be) so Lute could sneak out on the plane to the safety of anonymity outside before Millis discovered that the strychnine was flour?

And with that thought, which was conviction, too, Frank lunged to his feet, crashing the cot against the wall, and bellowed, "Millis!"

The talk out there died, and Millis came to the bars.

"Radio ahead and stop that plane! Tell the pilot to turn around and watch out for Lute Westock! He's your killer!"

"He's not on it," Millis said curtly. "I held him here as a material witness."

"Where is he?"

"At the hotel. He'll be over."

"Get him!" Frank raged. "He's your killer,

Millis, and he'll get away! You kept him off the plane. He's probably headed out of here by now!"

Millis said dryly, "You're a little slow on the uptake, Nearing. I figured you'd be hollering that either Charlie or Westock did it before I had the door locked on you."

"Listen to me," Frank said swiftly, harshly. "Go get him! Arrest him and hold him and I'll tell you how he did it!"

"I know how it was done," Millis said.

Frank gripped the timbers until his hands were white. Then he called to Charlie, "Go find out, Charlie! If he's in town, bring him here! Hurry!"

Charlie raced for the door. Millis watched him, a faint smile on his face. Kelcy was watching Frank with a strange intentness.

And then Frank began to talk. He explained swiftly, hurriedly, almost incoherently, how Lute could have done it. He told it all, about the letters and about Lute's story of dodging alimony. Millis listened politely, without any conviction in his face, and when Frank was finished Millis said, "And you expect me to believe he killed Bruce because Bruce knew about his dodging alimony?"

"That's just what I don't want you to believe!" Frank raged. "It was a stall, I tell you! Listen, Millis. I told you Lute was my partner! He wasn't! I was hiding him — for two thousand dollars, no questions asked."

"Interesting," Millis murmured dryly. He didn't believe it. He was remembering Lute's meeting with Frank at the plane that first day,

241

the inquiry over mutual friends.

And Frank knew he was, and despair seized him. His pleading glance shuttled to Kelcy, and he surprised the expression on her face of a woman who is listening to a breathless revelation.

"Maybe it's true," she said to Millis.

Millis shook his head. "Kelcy, I've listened to a hundred, two hundred men try to crawl out from under their guilt. It goes just like this. Some stories are good, some are bad. This is bad."

But Frank wasn't beaten. "Millis, listen to me. What are my rights, here? Can I send a radio message? If I can't, will you send one for me?"

"I will. What is it?"

"Radio Joe Phillips at Chalk River. Tell him to go to the police barracks and give them a minute description of Lute Westock. Tell him to ask them to look in their files, to broadcast his description, to find out if he's wanted. Ask him to check on a man named Carl, a lawyer, whom Lute knew. Will you do that?"

Millis said patiently, "I'll do it. I'll even sign it and send it to the police myself and ask them for Joe Phillips' confirmation. Is that all right?"

"It's fine," Frank said bitterly. "While you're at it, you might as well radio for some search planes, too, to help you find Westock after you get their answer."

"I know what their answer will be right now. It will read, 'Description vague. Send further details.' I'll wire them again, they'll wire me again. We'll swap a dozen wires until I call the whole thing off. But I'll send it."

There was the sound of someone running outside, and a moment later Charlie burst through the door. "He's gone!" he panted. "The dogs are gone, too!"

"All right, Millis," Frank whipped out. "What about it?"

Millis shrugged indifferently. "I'm being punished, that's all. Westock is sore because I broke off your deal, and —"

"What deal?"

"The deal you had with a mining promoter outside. He was going out to fix it up."

"I didn't have any deal hanging fire!" Frank raged. "He lied to you! Doesn't that prove it?"

Millis shook his head wearily. "Nearing, you just got through telling me you had an ore discovery. Are you trying to tell me now that Westock wasn't going out to get the backing to mine it?"

Frank groaned softly in a bleak and savage disgust.

Millis went on, "As I said, Westock was sore about it. He's probably headed up the Wailing, and is going to make me come after him."

"You fool!" Frank shouted. "You damned knot-headed fool! I tell you he's running away!"

"Where? Into the bush? Nonsense. Every man in the North knows that he can't win that game. He needs food, he needs shells. Whenever he hits a post, the police are waiting for him — if the planes don't find him."

Millis straightened up and sighed. When he spoke, his tone was curt, firm. "I've had enough of this, Nearing. I've told you what I'll do. I'll wire out to the Chalk River barracks about Westock. I'll send a man up for Westock tomorrow. I'll engage any high-power lawyer you want. But it all changes nothing. You're under arrest for the murder by poison of Bruce McIvor. You'll be tried, and take your medicine."

Frank knew it was hopeless. Anger didn't help, nothing helped. Nothing, absolutely nothing, could convince Millis. He was already convinced.

Frank asked, "May I have a word with Charlie alone?"

"Not alone. I'll go over in the corner where I can watch you. First, I'll have to search him."

Charlie came over, holding up his hands as he had seen men do in the movies. "Put 'em down, cowboy," Millis growled.

While the search went on, Kelcy came slowly over to the cell and looked at Frank. His eyes were filled with a wild despair, but when he looked at her his glance softened a little.

"I didn't kill Bruce, Kelcy. If I hang for it, I still didn't kill him."

"I believe that," Kelcy said, her voice curiously faltering.

Frank looked at her searchingly, hope creeping into his eyes. "But you told Millis about the letter. He said you wanted to hang me."

"I don't know why I did it, Frank!" Kelcy said passionately. "I'm so confused, so helpless!

244

Saul Chenard told me I should! I did it against my better judgment. But I'm wrong! Oh, Frank, I know you didn't do it now. I feel it, I'm sure of it, I — He's got to believe you!"

Frank looked wonderingly at her, understanding now what she had gone through and not hating her. He had never hated her. But her words now were conviction; she'd found herself, and he knew it and it filled him with a hot, fighting pride.

"Go home, Kelcy," he murmured. "I'll get out of here, so help me."

"Can I help?"

"Yes. Go home, and keep believing I didn't do it."

His hand was on the crossbar. Kelcy reached in and squeezed it, and then turned swiftly and went out.

Millis retreated to a far corner and Charlie came over.

Frank said softly, "Charlie, where's he headed?"

"The Barren Land. He'd have to. All the posts and the railways south will be watched."

"Can you find out for sure? They're our dogs he's got and our sled. You know the track they leave. The snow is new, and you might pick up some sign in the few hours of daylight left. Can you?"

"I'll try."

"If you can find anything we've got a chance. Now listen carefully, fella." His voice sank to a whisper and stayed there a long time. At the finish of it, Charlie nodded, did not smile, and left.

Chapter Twenty

The hours until supper that night were the longest Frank had ever spent. He lay on his cot, hearing Millis fussing with papers at his desk, and thought of Lute. Not of Lute's guilt, because he was certain of that, but of Lute's destination. Would Lute head south, for outside? Once there, of course, he could vanish. But it was ten days' travel by dog team to the end of steel, and another three days' travel on the train before he would be out of the bush. Would Lute figure that his secret could be kept that long? No. He wasn't a fool. He would figure that even with good luck it wouldn't take the police more than a few days to discover that the poison in Bruce's bottle was flour. After that, they'd broadcast his description and every post and especially the train would be watched closely. Going south, he'd walk into a trap.

That left east, west, and north, the bush country. And Frank didn't fool himself; Lute was a bushman. East or west, they'd be searching for him in planes, watching every post, quizzing Indians and trappers for any strange sign. Sooner or later they'd pick him up.

That left the north and the Barren Land. That was a country so big it couldn't be searched.

Only the hardiest and toughest men trapped it, and they went out in the summer and came back in the summer, with no town trips in between. A lonely, self-reliant type, they didn't give a damn about the law, which never reached them. Lute was safe among them until the summer, and then he could throw in with a roving family of Eskimos who seldom saw a post. When the talk died down, when he was given up for dead and the vigilance was relaxed, he could work south to freedom. It might take a couple of years, but it could be done. The only thing stopping him would be his lack of an outfit. In that bleak country where if a man missed the caribou herds he starved to death, an outfit was important, and Lute didn't have one. But if Lute hadn't stopped at murder here, he wouldn't stop at murder there. Barren Land trappers had outfits, and trappers could be killed for them. Lute was already facing death, and one more crime wouldn't make any difference.

Then there were the police to consider. They always got their man, so the books and movies said. But that was not true. The Royal Canadian Mounted Police was a fine body of men, perhaps the best police force in the world, but they were fallible. They didn't always get their man; they *almost* always did.

Those were the odds Lute faced — tough, but not impossible. And Frank was certain Lute would head down north. Charlie, with similar reasoning, thought so too. It was only a hunch, but the one they were going to play.

After supper, when Millis was in the office again, Charlie returned, his dark face inscrutable. He paused just inside the door again and asked Millis if he could talk with Frank — alone. Again Millis said yes, again searched him and retired to the far corner.

Charlie came up to the cell.

"Everything ready?" Frank murmured.

Charlie nodded.

"Play it fast," Frank said. "Now, give me the paper."

Charlie reached in his hip pocket and took out a paper, which he gave to Frank. Frank opened it and pretended to read it.

Then he said in a voice that Millis could hear, "But you ought to give it to him, Charlie."

"No," Charlie said.

"But he ought to see it. Let me give it to him, will you?"

Charlie pretended to hesitate, then shrugged.

"Take a look at this, Millis," Frank called. "Charlie found it in the wastebasket in Lute's hotel room."

Millis was curious. He came across the room to take the paper that Frank extended through the timber bars. He stood there beside Charlie, unfolding the paper.

Frank looked at Charlie and nodded. Charlie took a slow step to one side, putting Millis between him and the cell.

And then Charlie lunged, throwing the whole

weight of his body into Millis. Millis was taken by surprise. He went off balance and staggered back a step, and his broad shoulders hit the cell timbers with wall-shaking impact. Charlie pinned him solidly, his shoulder in Millis' chest. Millis slugged up at him, and then Frank's arms came through the bars. One arm wrapped around Millis' midriff, and his other hand settled over Millis' mouth. For five seconds, as Charlie backed off and set himself, Millis wrestled savagely, tearing at Frank's hands and heaving away from the timbers until Frank's arms strained in their sockets to hold him.

And then Charlie hit him. It was a blow on the jaw that cracked loud and sharp in the silence, and it drove Millis' head back against the timber bar with a vicious sledgehammer force. Frank felt Millis go limp under him, and he let him slowly down to the floor.

Silently Charlie rifled Millis' pockets until he found the key. Then he unlocked the door and Frank stepped out and knelt by Millis. He felt the back of Millis' head and murmured, "You hit him too hard, Charlie."

"I guess I did," Charlie admitted, and added mildly, "Damn him, anyway."

"Give a hand." They lifted Millis between them and lugged him into the cell and onto the cot. Charlie gave Frank a roll of tape, and while Frank taped Millis' mouth shut, Charlie uncoiled a length of small rope from around his waist. They trussed Millis securely, then stepped out and locked the cell again. Frank pocketed the key.

Frank quietly locked the door that let into the house while Charlie went outside. In a moment he returned with a fur cap, mittens, and parka, all new. Frank donned them and then blew out the lamp, turned the lock on the door, and stepped out into the clear cold night.

Charlie led the way to the darkened road. Fifty yards away from the house two dog teams were waiting — one Bruce's dogs, which Charlie brought down days ago from Swan Lake and had been feeding up at the hotel before he returned them, the other his own light team.

"Your outfit's in my sled," Charlie said. "I fed the dogs two hours ago and you've got two days' dog feed with you. When you hit the fur portage, keep north. You'll see a trail turning east, but it's a wood trail, not Lute's." He hesitated. "He's got a five-hour start on you, Frank, but he'll have to break trail."

"His dogs are heavier, but mine are faster," Frank countered.

"As soon as Millis has followed me up to the shack, the planes will be out, remember."

"Lute will figure that out. He'll have to keep to the bush, too."

"A few days of that and he'll take to his shoes. So will you. Then's the time to watch him, Frank."

"Sure."

There was an awkward pause, and Charlie said, "If I'm lucky, they won't find Millis till eleven

250

or so. It'll take another hour to get him loose and round up an outfit. You think he'll figure my trail is yours and follow me?"

"I dunno. He thinks Lute's up there, and that I'll head for Lute. It's worth the trouble."

"I guess."

There was a longer pause then, and Charlie blurted out, "Damn it, Frank, be careful."

They shook hands briefly, and Frank untied the tail rope. He spoke quietly to Charlie's dogs, who loafed into motion. Once clear of Millis' house, he took out the whip and cracked it once. The dogs broke into a long lope as they skirted the town, hit the river, and headed for the fur portage.

Somewhere out there, Lute was bulling it through the night, trying to put as much distance between himself and Lobstick as he could.

The second day out, Frank heard the first plane. He was two hundred yards out on the bald surface of a small lake when he heard it, and panic seized him. He shouted at the dogs in a wild voice and they raced for the portage at which he was aiming.

Once on land among the trees, he hawed the dogs off the trail under some screening spruce, and then stood there panting, listening. The plane was closer now, but still far distant.

Moving to the edge of the spruce, he scanned the sky. Luck had been with him so far — and with Lute — for this morning, the morning they were most likely to start the search, the sky was overcast.

In these two days since he left, the trails around Lobstick would have grown numerous and confusing. Added to that bit of luck was the overcast sky, which would not throw shadows visible to a plane. That meant the searchers up there must wait for a clear sky, when the early or late sun laid its blue shadows on the edge of the trail to guide the searchers. And, unless the weather was deceiving, a snow was due shortly. That would finish covering up the trail. The only thing left to the planes then was a tour in an ever widening circle, running down the trails of every trapper in the bush.

Frank saw the plane at last. It was far to the east, heading north in a straight line. Someone was playing a hunch, a wrong hunch. Frank gnawed on a piece of half-frozen bannock and eyed Charlie's dogs critically. They were a tough bunch, but not so tough as his own team, which Lute was driving. They had speed, but not so much stamina as his own, and right now it was speed he wanted. For Lute was having to break trail, while Frank traveled faster on the trail Lute had already broken. A snow would change that. It would mean that his fast trail was gone, and he was on equal terms with Lute, who had the better dogs.

When the plane had gone, Frank swung his team onto the trail again and set out. Now he could judge how far Lute was ahead of him, for Lute would have ducked into the brush just as he had. It was four hours later when he came to the spot where Lute had pulled off a bare trail into the bush. That meant Frank had cut Lute's head start down from five hours to four.

That was not good. He should have done better. It meant, of course, that Lute was pushing his dogs, Frank's dogs, to their very limit.

It began to snow soon afterward, and Frank watched it glumly in the gone day. It was time to camp, but he ignored that. He was putting his dogs to their first test. A smart leader could smell out a snow-covered trail, and it was important that he find out if this leader was smart, for much hinged on it. If he was smart, it meant night travel.

Three hours later in that snow-piling darkness, Frank had his answer, and it was given to him in the moiling, wind-scoured dark of a big lake. He came across a fresh trail — a too fresh trail — and knew it for his own. The wind hadn't been shifting to all points of the compass, as he thought; Charlie's dogs had circled.

Frank put them north, kept them there by the wind, and an hour later made his late camp on the shore. Tomorrow, he knew, he would lose an hour finding Lute's trail, and from here on it would be slow and heavy work. He fed his dogs half rations, himself less than half, and rolled into his bedroll, tasting his first discouragement. From now until the snow ceased he and Lute would travel long hours at the same speed and with the same trail conditions, keeping that same ten or twelve miles between them. And only when the snow stopped and he picked up Lute's broken trail again would he have his second chance to overtake him.

It snowed for five long days. Frank trailed Lute by instinct then, for Lute's trail, a faint rounded groove in the snow's surface, was drifted over by the wind. He was having to watch the trail closely now for dog feed — the carcasses of the game that Lute was sure to have to kill if he wanted to keep his dogs alive.

And in that bleak succession of lonely days, the pursuit settled into a chess game in Frank's mind. He could plot it out, move for move. He had to turn up Lute's trail patiently, which slowed him, and Lute had to take time out to hunt, which slowed him. Lute would pull ahead for a few days, then he would run out of dog feed and have to hunt. Then Frank would whittle down Lute's lead, but never enough. When he got to the carcass it might still be warm deep inside, but Lute would be hours gone. And Frank would have to slog along at his snail's pace, losing the trail and finding it while Lute increased his lead.

When the snow finally fell off and the sun broke out, the planes were at it again. Frank counted three on the eighth day. For four hours of daylight on that day he huddled with his dogs under the inadequate screen of some scrub tamarack. He was hungry all the time now, for his bannock had given out and his flour was gone and he was living on meat, like his dogs. Two meals a day of boiled meat, one before daylight and one after daylight so the smoke of his fires wouldn't show, was not enough. He could see what lay ahead of him as he huddled there with his dogs that day and heard the planes wing over in their remorseless hunt. It was a bleak prospect.

The bush was thinning out, making it harder to hide his trail under the shore trees. And every hour of the day he was listening for those planes, his nerves drawing wire thin, his belly gnawing with hunger. Soon, maybe tomorrow, he would come to a spot where his trail couldn't be hidden, and he'd have to take to the thinning bush, casting back at night for Lute's trail. That might work until the next snow. But after that, he couldn't do it. He couldn't drive his dogs miles off the trail for the shelter of the bush, and then expect to pick up Lute's trail after dark.

He looked across the blazing white lake stretched out in front of him. A month from now, a man could see mirages on this lake, just as if it were desert. Now it was lonely as the cold stars he would see tonight. Somewhere off there, huddled under some trees, was Lute, watching the airplanes with his patient, cunning eyes. In the tough core of Lute's mind was an indomitableness that would win for him. Soon, Lute would know that nobody could be following him, and then he'd be safe. He'd hole up in one camp, not giving the planes a trail to guide them, and wait for them to give up.

For a long and bitter hour, Frank cast up his own chances, and they were slim. He was licked by Lute's dogs, not by his bush knowledge or his strength or his stubbornness or his will. He was licked by dogs, which were tougher and better than these courageous dogs by his side.

It came to him then that a gamble might do it. If he failed, he was finished and might as well turn back. But it was his only chance of success.

When the planes droned off, Frank put his tired dogs onto the lake again, hugging the shore. In midafternoon he came across the carcass of a caribou calf that Lute had killed the day before. Frank took a quarter and went on, turning over his plan in his mind.

The first step was to reach the far end of the lake, cross the portage, and see what lay beyond, and he'd have to do it during the daylight. His trail be damned! He'd have to take the chance of laying it out across the lake for the planes to spot.

He cut across the lake for the upper portage, pushing his dogs, using his whip. Out on the lake the snow was drifted hard, and he drove his dogs mercilessly through that afternoon, keeping an eye out for planes and silently praying that they wouldn't catch him out here in the open.

His dogs would be done at the end of this day, he could see that. And he didn't care. The narrow strip of black ahead that announced the portage grew taller and finally took on the green cast of conifers. He reached land as the late sun was wheeling into the west. It was hurry now, and hurry fast. On the portage he found Lute's camp of the night before. It was the first camp he'd found in days that wasn't snowed over, and he knew it for last night's.

He reached the far end of the two-mile portage at the fading of daylight. His dogs dropped in their tracks as he walked past them to look at the lake. His heart beat faster at the sight that greeted him.

This lake was long, its far shore out of sight. Crossing that lake meant a day's travel for Lute, considering the time he had had to hide today. He'd be camped at its upper portage tonight.

Frank unhooked his dogs, did not chain them, laid the last of the dog feed where they could get it, cut off a chunk for himself and put it in his parka pocket, then brought out his snow-shoes.

As the last light died in the west, he stepped out onto the lake, rifle over his shoulder. He had from now until daylight, fourteen hours, in which to overtake Lute. The trail Lute had broken that day would do him no good, for Lute had clung to the shore line. Frank was cutting across. And if he failed — well, if he failed . . .

The night was clear, and Frank's mind settled into that timeless, stupid, and unthinking blank that comes to a man long alone and physically tired. He remembered little of it, except that he watched the Big Dipper wheel in that cold sky, silently ticking off the hours he had left. He was beyond tiredness, and his walking was almost a reflex action.

It was some time after six o'clock, after twelve hours of walking, that he saw the funneling shore line loom up in the night ahead of him. He stopped, too tired to do anything but gaze stupidly at the shore. Was Lute camped there somewhere on this portage? How would he approach him? His dogs would be chained around him, and dogs always wakened at this hour of the morning, the coldest, to stretch and whine and shift their position.

Then stay off the trail, he told himself. Circle him. Take your time. You've got an hour till daylight.

From some deep well of stubborn strength, Frank called up enough reserve to get moving again. When he reached shore, he kicked out of his snowshoes and sank to his knees in the loose snow. It was work, agony, to walk without them, but they were too noisy. He wallowed on into the bush, staggering with weariness, and entered the trees as quietly as night falling.

The portage, like all these other portages, was a low strip of land between two lakes joined by a stream. Somewhere along that stream, Lute would be camped.

Frank pushed on. He kept high on the slope, for his scent would rise above the dogs. The night in here was thick black vellum. Slowly, cautiously, he worked his way angling down the slope, seeing nothing and yet stubbornly keeping on, not knowing if the portage were a hundred yards wide or a mile.

258

He'd have to hurry. Lute would be ready to travel by daylight. He felt the lip of a rock ledge under him now, running parallel to the stream that must be off there. He traveled it slowly, feeling his way deeper and deeper into the portage. A crawling fear was in him now, and he knew it was of his own making, bred by his own stealth. And suddenly, the futility of what he was doing came to him. There was nobody here. He was sneaking up on a phantom of his own mind.

He hunkered down there in the snow and hung his head, beaten and bone-weary and not even angry. And then a noise seeped into his consciousness, and he raised his head. He was imagining it, but he listened until he could hear the blood pumping through his veins. And then it came again, off to the left and below him, the thin and quavering whine of a dog that has been overworked and underfed and is dismally cold.

All the weariness fell away, and he sat there immobile, his blood on fire. Gently he rose, more gently took a step to his left along the ledge. And another. He waited then, and the sound didn't come again. He took another step and then he squatted again. He was miserably cold now, yet he was afraid to move lest he alarm the camp. He was close, very close, he thought.

He would have to wait, even if his inactivity meant frost-bitten fingers and toes, until Lute rose and made a fire.

He sat there fifteen minutes, twenty minutes, staring at that blackness. And presently he realized

259

that it was getting lighter. He could make out trees, a gray-black smear of snow in a clearing below him.

And then he knew something was wrong. If it was daylight, Lute should be up! All his instinct warned him to be careful, to draw back.

He came slowly erect and took a step backward, and then something slashed him in the shoulder and slammed him around and the flat crack of a rifle filled the night. He fell on his side, hearing the boiling and immediate barking of the startled dogs.

Lute had been waiting for him! Lute had expected him!

The snow was deep where he fell, and he was hidden. To rise was to die, and he knew it. Besides, he didn't know where Lute was. And then he did the only thing he could.

He made a faint gagging sound and lay still. The seconds ribboned on. Again the rifle cracked. He heard the slug slap the stone beyond his head. He lay utterly still, waiting for the third slug that would drive the life out of him. His shoulder was numb, didn't hurt. And it was quiet. Even the dogs, silenced by fear, were voiceless.

Then came an uneasy whine, and on top of that the thump, thump of a dog's tail on the frozen snow.

That meant Lute was moving, passing a dog, coming toward him. Frank's rifle was still in his hand. He couldn't cock it, or the noise would give him away. He grasped it firmly, then slowly turned his head toward the rim of the ledge, panic chilling him. He couldn't lie here and let Lute put his gun over the ledge and shoot him.

He raised his head then in the half-light. Four feet away, he saw six inches of Lute's gun, barrel waving upright as Lute would hold it to climb the steep slope. Frank rolled his body and swung his gun like a club over the ledge.

It crashed into Lute's gun with a metallic clang, and then into Lute, and Frank's momentum carried him over the ledge and down the slope.

Lute had gone over backward, and he fell and rolled, too. Fear driving him, Frank cocked his gun as he skidded to a stop in the moiling snow.

Lute's gun crashed out again, and Frank came to his knees, hearing Lute lever in yet another shell. The place that sound came from was a gray blur against the trees, and Frank in his panic held his rifle out like a pistol and pointed it at the spot and pulled the trigger. The rifle kicked up and he tried to raise his left arm to steady it and his arm wouldn't move. Moaning, he rolled over in the snow and got the gun between his legs and levered in a shell and came fighting to his knees.

And only then did he realize Lute had not shot again. Frank waited there on his knees, snow in his eyes and mouth, and sought for that gray blur. It wasn't there, and the dogs were barking savagely.

Slowly he staggered to his feet and lunged over to Lute and dropped beside him. Lute's face was only a blur to him, half buried in the snow. He could hear Lute's breath bubbling out, and he reached out and pushed him on his back. Lute raised a hand to strike at him, but he couldn't make it. His hand fell to his side, and his breath bubbled and gurgled.

Frank knelt there a long minute as Lute's face took shape in the half-light of dawn.

"Lute, Lute!" Frank called hoarsely.

Lute opened his eyes. He stared blankly at Frank, and then turned his head away.

"Lute, why did you do it? Lute!"

Lute moved his head imperceptibly in negation and then shut his eyes. Seconds later the bubbling faded off, and he died.

Chapter Twenty-one

Frank got a fire going first, and then laggingly peeled off his clothes by its warmth to look at his wound. It was in his shoulder, and it was seeping blood and beginning to come to life with a fiery and savage throbbing. Under his fingers, he could feel the bone moving. But now he had to stop the bleeding. Lute had a little flour left. Frank plastered it to the hole, fistful after fistful, until it clotted and plugged the wound. Afterward, he took the meat from his parka pocket, impaled it on a stick, and while his breakfast was cooking, dragged in all the wood, rotten and otherwise, that he could find.

He went over to look at Lute again, impelled by a dull and passionless curiosity. His bullet had caught Lute in the chest. Death's nobility was not in his face; it was shrunken and gaunt and implacable, and it meant nothing to Frank. It betrayed something, though — the fear that had been riding Lute during these past days. More proof of that lay in the camp, for Lute's bed beside the fire consisted of a single dark blanket made up to look like a bed. His real bedroll from which he had roused was on the other side of the fire in the brush.

Frank ate and talked to the dogs to hear the

sound of his voice, and then in the clear bright morning he threw the rotten logs on the fire. They lifted a blue smoke high into the still air. Afterward he rolled up in Lute's bedroll to wait in an unthinking and brain-beaten weariness.

In the midmorning he heard the first plane. He got up to watch it, and knew immediately that the pilot had spotted his smoke. The noise of the motor grew louder, and then he caught sight of the plane circling and losing altitude. The sound faded, and then it grew stronger and stronger, and presently the plane came over him, just above the treetops, banked a little so the spotters could see out. Frank waved his arm and gave them a good view of him.

The plane vanished, and the noise faded off and after a long wait he heard it returning again. It was taxiing on the lake.

Then the motor settled into an idling hum, and Frank dropped weakly on the bedroll, dully observing the camp. Well, he'd got Lute, and now they'd get him. There were no witnesses. Nothing was changed, except justice had been done.

It turned out to be Millis who led the three men that tramped into the camp. Millis looked at Frank and didn't smile and said, "Did you get him?"

Frank gestured to the brush where Lute lay, and then hung his head wearily. The three of them, all police, Frank supposed, went immediately to Lute. Afterward Millis came over to him. His face was red with cold, his blue eyes bright as glass.

"You're hurt!" Millis said abruptly, noting his bloody parka.

"Shot in the shoulder. It isn't bleeding, and I can wait till we get in. Will you bring the dogs?" He thought of something and looked up at Millis and said, "I know I won't need them, but Charlie will — after he gets out of jail for slugging you."

"Sure," Millis said. He helped Frank to his feet, then called to the three other men to bring Lute's body and the dogs.

Frank could hardly stand up, but he made it across the short portage to the plane. He was put on the seat beside the pilot, and Millis and the pilot left him and went back to camp. Presently they reappeared with Lute's body and the dogs, which were all loaded in.

Frank told the pilot about Charlie's team and considered his duty done. He sat in the seat, feeling sick and weary and dead as the plane took off.

Suddenly a hand holding a whisky bottle was thrust in front of him. "Take a big long jolt," Millis said. "It'll prepare you for the news."

Frank did. The whisky felt first like ice water, and then exploded into a warm heat in his stomach, coursing through his veins like gentle snakes.

"Ready?" Millis asked.

Frank nodded, and Millis thrust a folded paper in his hands. It was a radiogram, and it read:

LEON WESTPHAL, ALIAS LUTHER WEST-
OCK, WANTED FOR SABOTAGE EXPLO-
SION AT CHALK RIVER PLANT IN WHICH
FIVE KILLED AND PLANT WRECKED OCT.
16. CARL BARIOSOV, ALIAS CARL BARRIE,
CHALK RIVER BOOKKEEPER AND ACCOM-
PLICE, CONFESSED ON ARREST THROUGH
YOUR ADVICE. BARIOSOV AND WESTPHAL
COMMUNIST AGENTS. JOE PHILLIPS NOT.
WHY QUERY?

MCCLEOD, CHALK RIVER

Frank read it twice and yet a third time, too
weary to be surprised, and he heard Millis' low
chuckle behind him. When he turned, the other
two officers were smiling at him.

"So he's the partner you took for two thousand
dollars?" Millis said. "You've learned something."

"Yes," Frank said slowly.

"Westock's score altogether was eight," Millis
continued. "Your Charlie, on his way to draw
us off your trail up the Wailing, turned something
up at Swan Lake. Trust an Indian; the trail didn't
look right. He found Bonnie Tucker, number six,
dumped in a sulphur spring. And since it was
Bonnie that was wanted when Mary Paulin was
shot, we'll raise the count to seven. Bruce McIvor
makes eight."

"But why did he kill Bonnie?"

"Saul Chenard's guess is that he thought she
knew the same thing Bruce knew. By the way,
you needn't be shy about where that strychnine

266

came from. Kelcy told me. I've got Saul in jail, due for a put-away for wholesale strychnine peddling."

Frank turned further around to see Millis' face. At that moment his shoulder gave him a twinge that drained the blood out of his face and made him forget all of it.

At the hospital in Lobstick, which they reached two hours later, Doc Hardy gave Frank another drink and examined and cleaned his shoulder.

"You deserve to die for putting that flour in there," Doc Hardy said scathingly. "But I'm not going to kill you. You're going out to a surgeon who knows more about bone splinters than I do."

"We've got a plane he can lie down in due back in twenty minutes," a strange police officer said. "Can he wait?"

"If he goes in the hospital and lies down. Want another drink, Nearing?"

Frank took it. Doc Hardy led him to one of the four beds in his hospital, and Frank sank on it.

He heard voices out in the office, and then Millis, Kelcy, and Charlie came in. He understood Charlie's proud grin and replied with one of his own, and then he regarded Kelcy. There was a high excitement in her blue eyes and a pleasure in her face that almost glowed.

"Doc Hardy says you're a poor case," Kelcy said. "Not worth bothering with."

Millis had gone to close the door and now he came over to the bedside. His expression was grave as he regarded Frank.

"A man's got to live with his conscience," he began, "so I might as well start." There was a long troubled pause, and then he spoke in an ironic tone of voice. "They think I'm something out at headquarters. They figure I broke this case. That radiogram you told me to send to Chalk River turned the trick. And then there was that plane that I wouldn't let Westock take. That's to my credit too. Your jail break was just tough luck, they think. And I hope I die if this isn't the truth, but they've forgiven me for assuming that the flour was strychnine. All in all, I'm quite a fair-headed lad, and they think I'm something special."

His voice trailed off, and he was regarding Frank with a stubborn honesty. His broad face, high-colored with the cold he had been in during the week of search, looked rugged and craggy and kind, as Frank remembered it before all this trouble. His tunic fitted him snugly; he looked like a man whose shrewdness or job would never alter his conviction that people were to be pitied and helped. And Frank was suddenly aware that Millis was asking advice and asking it humbly in front of his friends. He wanted to know if he should tell his superiors the whole truth.

"Let them think it," Frank said. "A man accepts his luck, doesn't he? Besides, I think you're a damn good police officer, Millis. One of the best."

Millis looked at him searchingly and then the

268

old grin broke his face.

"So do I," he agreed.

He took Charlie out with him, and Kelcy sat on the edge of the bed, holding Frank's hand in hers. Frank wondered if he were a little drunk, watching her. He concluded that drunk or sober, tired or fresh, he would think her about the loveliest girl he knew.

He said, "We got off to a bad start, didn't we? And don't say that means a good finish. It's good and you don't have to say it."

"You were a bear," Kelcy said. "Come to think of it, I was something of a dirty-nosed little tramp myself."

"Agreed." Frank grimaced. "The trouble with me was I had a bad case of wanting gold in my pockets."

"Are you ashamed of that?"

"Not a bit. I'm explaining — apologizing, maybe, for something I've neglected. And that's you, my dear."

"I could use a little bit of nonneglect. I'll confess it, and not be coy."

They sat in silence a moment, looking at each other without troubling to talk. They were new and different to each other, and it was almost like a discovery.

"I've been thinking," Kelcy said. "Would you like me to go out with you?"

"I was coming to that," Frank said. "Coming fast, too."

Kelcy said soberly, "It'll be a long stretch in

the hospital for you, Doc says. I'd miss you if I stayed. I've just discovered that the last week hasn't been any fun."

"I know a place —" Frank began lazily, dreamily.

Kelcy leaned over and kissed him. "You can tell me that on the plane, Frank. I'll be back as soon as I can get another dress and a comb."

Frank watched her go out. His shoulder was hurting and he was a little drunk, he thought, and yet he'd never felt better.

The employees of G.K. HALL hope you have enjoyed this Large Print book. All our Large Print titles are designed for easy reading, and all our books are made to last. Other G.K. Hall Large Print books are available at your library, through selected bookstores, or directly from us. For more information about current and up-coming titles, please call or mail your name and address to:

G.K. HALL
PO Box 159
Thorndike, Maine 04986
800/223-6121
207/948-2962